# Whistleblower

## Political, Volume 2

Nicholas Andrew Martinez

Published by Harmony House Publishing, 2024.

WHISTLEBLOWER

**First edition. November 24, 2024.**

Copyright © 2024 Nicholas Andrew Martinez.

ISBN: 979-8230071884

Written by Nicholas Andrew Martinez.

# Table of Contents

To the courageous whistleblowers, past, present, and future, who risk everything to bring truth to light. Your bravery inspires us all.

And to the tireless journalists and advocates who stand by them, unwavering in your pursuit of justice and transparency. This story is for you.

May we all strive to live with integrity and the courage to make a difference.

# Chapter 1: The Discovery

The humming of fluorescent lights overhead and the quiet tapping of keyboards provided the usual backdrop for a day at Meridian Technologies, a leading government contractor. Lisa Bennett, a mid-level employee, sat at her desk surrounded by stacks of papers and two computer screens displaying various documents and spreadsheets. Her brown hair was tied back in a neat ponytail, and her glasses perched on her nose, reflecting the screen's glow.

Lisa had worked at Meridian for nearly five years. She was known for her meticulous attention to detail and her ability to navigate the bureaucratic complexities of government contracts. Her role involved managing compliance and ensuring that all projects adhered to federal regulations—a job that required a keen eye and a strong sense of integrity.

It was a typical Wednesday afternoon when Lisa's routine was disrupted. She was reviewing a series of documents related to a high-profile defense contract when she noticed something odd. One of the expense reports contained entries that seemed unusually high. Curious, she decided to dig deeper.

She cross-referenced the report with the original invoices and purchase orders. As she compared the figures, her brow furrowed in confusion. The numbers didn't add up. Lisa continued to investigate, her curiosity piqued by the discrepancies.

After hours of painstakingly examining the documents, Lisa stumbled upon a series of transactions that raised red flags. The amounts were exorbitant, and the descriptions were vague. Several invoices were marked for "consulting services," but there were no details about the nature of the services provided or the consultants involved. Additionally, the payments were made to shell companies with obscure names and offshore accounts.

Lisa's heart began to race as she realized the implications of what she had uncovered. These transactions were not just errors or anomalies—they were deliberate acts of corruption. The more she delved into the documents, the clearer the picture became. High-ranking government officials and corporate executives were involved in a massive scheme to siphon off taxpayer money through fraudulent contracts and kickbacks.

As the gravity of the situation sank in, Lisa felt a wave of nausea. She leaned back in her chair, staring at the screen in disbelief. She knew she had stumbled upon something significant, something that could potentially bring down powerful figures and expose widespread corruption.

But with that realization came a heavy burden. Lisa was acutely aware of the risks involved in exposing the truth. Whistleblowers often faced severe repercussions—job loss, legal battles, harassment, and even threats to their safety. She had heard stories of people who had tried to do the right thing, only to have their lives turned upside down.

Lisa's mind raced with conflicting thoughts. On one hand, she felt a moral obligation to expose the corruption and hold those responsible accountable. On the other hand, she feared for her job, her safety, and the impact it would have on her life. She had worked hard to build her career at Meridian, and the thought of losing everything was terrifying.

She thought about her family—her parents, who had always been supportive and proud of her achievements, and her younger brother, who looked up to her as a role model. How would they react if she became embroiled in a scandal? How would she explain the situation to them?

As the hours ticked by, Lisa sat in her cubicle, grappling with the moral dilemma. She knew that keeping silent would make her complicit in the corruption, but speaking out could destroy her life. The weight of the decision pressed down on her, making it difficult to breathe.

Finally, she made a decision. She couldn't ignore what she had found. Her conscience wouldn't allow it. She had to take action, but she needed to be smart about it. Lisa knew she couldn't do this alone—she needed help from someone with the expertise and resources to investigate the matter thoroughly and ensure her safety.

Her mind turned to Jake Harrison, a renowned investigative journalist known for his tenacity and dedication to exposing corruption. Jake had a reputation for taking on powerful adversaries and uncovering the truth, no matter the cost. Lisa had followed his work for years, admiring his courage and determination.

She took a deep breath and pulled out her phone. With trembling fingers, she searched for Jake's contact information. She found his email address and typed out a message, carefully outlining the basics of what she had discovered. She didn't include too many details, fearing that her email might be intercepted. Instead, she requested a meeting to discuss the matter in person.

Lisa hesitated for a moment before hitting send. She knew there was no turning back now. She had taken the first step toward exposing the truth, and she hoped that Jake would be able to help her navigate the treacherous path ahead.

The next few days were a blur of anxiety and anticipation. Lisa continued to go to work, trying to maintain a semblance of normalcy while she waited for Jake's response. Every time her phone buzzed with a new email or message, her heart skipped a beat.

Finally, an email from Jake appeared in her inbox. Lisa's hands shook as she opened it. The message was brief but reassuring. Jake had agreed to meet her and had suggested a discreet location—a small café on the outskirts of the city. He assured her that he would take all necessary precautions to ensure their meeting was secure.

On the day of the meeting, Lisa dressed in a simple blouse and jeans, hoping to blend in and avoid drawing attention to herself. She arrived at the café early, choosing a table near the back where they would have some privacy. As she waited, she sipped on a cup of herbal tea, her nerves on edge.

A few minutes later, Jake walked in. He was taller than she had expected, with a rugged demeanor and a piercing gaze that seemed to see right through her. He wore a casual jacket and jeans, looking every bit the seasoned journalist he was.

"Lisa?" he asked, approaching her table.

"Yes," she replied, standing to shake his hand. "Thank you for meeting with me."

Jake nodded and took a seat across from her. "I read your email. It sounds like you've uncovered something significant. Can you tell me more about what you found?"

Lisa took a deep breath and began to recount her discovery, explaining the discrepancies in the expense reports and the suspicious transactions she had uncovered. She handed over copies of the documents she had brought with her, watching as Jake examined them with a practiced eye.

"This is damning evidence," Jake said, his tone serious. "If what you're saying is true, this could be one of the biggest corruption scandals in recent history. But we need to be careful. The people involved in this are powerful and won't hesitate to retaliate."

Lisa nodded, her heart pounding. "I know the risks, but I can't just ignore what I found. I need your help to expose this and protect myself."

Jake leaned back in his chair, considering her words. "I'll help you, but we need to proceed cautiously. I'll start by verifying the documents and gathering additional evidence. We'll need to build an airtight case before we go public. In the meantime, you need to be very careful. Don't talk about this with anyone at work, and take steps to protect your digital footprint."

Lisa agreed, feeling a mix of relief and trepidation. She knew that the road ahead would be difficult, but she also knew that she had made the right decision. With Jake's help, she would expose the corruption and hold those responsible accountable.

Over the next few weeks, Jake and his team worked tirelessly to investigate the corruption scheme. They dug deeper into the financial records, interviewed potential whistleblowers, and followed the money trail to its source. Lisa continued to provide them with information, discreetly passing along documents and insights while maintaining her cover at work.

As the investigation progressed, Lisa's anxiety grew. She felt like she was constantly looking over her shoulder, fearing that someone would discover what she was doing. She took extra precautions, using encrypted communication methods and avoiding any behavior that might raise suspicion.

Despite the stress and fear, Lisa found solace in her growing partnership with Jake. He was a steady presence, offering reassurance and guidance as they navigated the complexities of the investigation. They developed a deep trust and camaraderie, united by their shared commitment to exposing the truth.

One evening, as Lisa was leaving work, she noticed a black SUV parked across the street. It was the same vehicle she had seen several times over the past few days. Her heart raced as she realized she was being followed. She quickly changed her route, taking a circuitous path to shake off her pursuers.

When she arrived home, Lisa locked the door behind her and took a moment to collect herself. She knew that the danger was real and that she needed to stay vigilant. She contacted Jake, informing him of the situation.

"We need to escalate our security measures," Jake said, his voice tense. "I'll arrange for someone to keep an eye on your house and make sure you're not followed. We can't afford to take any chances."

Lisa agreed, grateful for Jake's support. The stakes were higher than ever, but she was determined to see this through. She knew that the truth had to come out, no matter the cost.

As the weeks turned into months, the investigation continued to gain momentum. Jake's team uncovered more evidence, linking the corruption scheme to high-ranking government officials and corporate executives. The scope of the scandal was staggering, involving millions of dollars in fraudulent contracts and kickbacks.

Lisa's role as a whistleblower became increasingly precarious. She continued to work at Meridian, maintaining her cover and providing Jake with valuable information. She felt a constant sense of tension, knowing that at any moment, her secret could be discovered.

One evening, as Lisa was preparing to leave work, she received a call from Jake. "We have enough evidence to go public," he said. "But we need to plan our next steps carefully. Once we publish the story, there will be a backlash, and we need to be prepared."

Lisa took a deep breath, feeling a mix of relief and apprehension. "I'm ready. Let's do this."

Jake outlined their plan, detailing how they would release the information and ensure Lisa's safety. They would publish a series of articles, gradually revealing the extent of the corruption and the identities of those involved. Jake's team would work closely with law enforcement to secure warrants and arrests, ensuring that the culprits faced justice.

The day of the first publication arrived. Lisa sat at her desk, her heart pounding as she watched the clock. She knew that once the article was released, there would be no turning back. She took a deep breath and braced herself for the storm that was about to come.

At exactly noon, Jake published the first article. The headline was bold and damning, exposing the corruption scheme and implicating high-ranking officials and corporate executives. The article included excerpts from the documents Lisa had uncovered, as well as testimonies from other whistleblowers who had come forward.

The reaction was immediate and explosive. News outlets across the country picked up the story, and social media was abuzz with outrage and calls for accountability. The public demanded answers, and pressure mounted on the government and Meridian Technologies to respond.

Lisa watched the unfolding drama with a mix of satisfaction and fear. She knew that the truth was finally out, but she also knew that the backlash would be swift and severe. She received a call from Jake, who reassured her that they were taking all necessary precautions to protect her.

"Stay strong, Lisa," Jake said. "We're in this together. The truth is out, and there's no stopping it now."

As the days passed, the fallout from the publication continued to escalate. Government officials and corporate executives issued denials and attempted to discredit the investigation, but the evidence was overwhelming. Law enforcement agencies launched investigations, and several high-profile arrests were made.

Lisa's life was turned upside down. She was placed under protective custody, and her movements were closely monitored to ensure her safety. She felt a mix of relief and anxiety, knowing that her actions had made a significant impact but also fearing the repercussions.

The media frenzy showed no signs of abating. Jake's team continued to publish articles, each one revealing more damning evidence and further implicating the corrupt network. The public's demand for justice grew louder, and the pressure on the government and Meridian Technologies intensified.

One evening, as Lisa was watching the news, she received a call from Jake. "We've done it," he said, his voice filled with triumph. "The corruption network is collapsing, and the people responsible are being brought to justice. Your bravery and determination have made all the difference."

Lisa felt a wave of emotion wash over her. She had risked everything to expose the truth, and now, her efforts were paying off. The corrupt officials and executives who had abused their power were being held accountable, and a sense of justice was beginning to prevail.

As the weeks turned into months, the investigation continued to yield results. More arrests were made, and additional whistleblowers came forward, bolstered by Lisa's example. The government enacted new regulations to prevent future corruption, and Meridian Technologies faced significant consequences for its role in the scandal.

Lisa's life gradually began to return to a semblance of normalcy. She continued to work closely with Jake and his team, providing support and guidance to other whistleblowers. She found solace in the knowledge that she had made a difference and helped to bring about positive change.

One evening, as Lisa sat in her living room, she received a call from her parents. They had seen the news and were proud of her bravery and determination. Her younger brother, who had always looked up to her, expressed his admiration for her courage.

"We're so proud of you, Lisa," her mother said, her voice filled with emotion. "You've done something incredible, and we're here to support you every step of the way."

Lisa felt a sense of gratitude and relief. She had feared that her actions would alienate her from her family, but instead, they had brought them closer together. She knew that she had made the right decision, and she was ready to face whatever challenges lay ahead.

As she looked out at the city skyline, Lisa felt a renewed sense of purpose. The journey had been long and difficult, but she had emerged stronger and more determined than ever. She knew that the fight for justice was far from over, but she was ready to continue the battle, knowing that the truth had the power to change the world.

With Jake and her newfound allies by her side, Lisa embarked on the next chapter of her life. She was no longer just a mid-level employee at a government contractor—she was a symbol of courage and integrity, a whistleblower who had stood up against corruption and helped to bring about a new era of transparency and accountability. The road ahead was uncertain, but Lisa was ready to face it head-on, knowing that her actions had made a lasting impact and inspired others to do the same.

# Chapter 2: The Decision

L isa Bennett's discovery of massive corruption at Meridian Technologies left her with a profound sense of unease and moral conflict. The weight of what she had uncovered pressed down on her, making it difficult to focus on anything else. Every time she closed her eyes, she saw the incriminating documents, the fraudulent transactions, and the names of powerful figures implicated in the scandal.

For days, Lisa wrestled with her conscience. She knew that remaining silent would make her complicit in the corruption, but speaking out could jeopardize her career, her safety, and her entire life. She needed to confide in someone she could trust, someone with the expertise and resources to investigate and expose the truth.

Late one night, as she sat in her small apartment, surrounded by printouts and notes, Lisa made a decision. She couldn't do this alone. She needed help from someone who had a track record of taking on powerful adversaries and uncovering the truth. She needed Jake Harrison.

Jake Harrison was a renowned investigative journalist with a reputation for fearlessness and integrity. He had exposed numerous high-profile corruption cases and was known for his meticulous attention to detail and relentless pursuit of justice. Lisa had followed his work for years, admiring his courage and dedication.

With trembling hands, Lisa opened her laptop and began drafting an email to Jake. She outlined the basics of what she had discovered, careful not to include too many details that could be traced back to her. She requested a meeting, explaining that she had information of critical importance that needed to be shared in person.

Dear Mr. Harrison,

My name is Lisa Bennett, and I work at Meridian Technologies. I have recently uncovered evidence of significant corruption and illegal activities involving high-ranking government officials and corporate executives. The implications are far-reaching, and I believe that the public needs to know the truth.

I would like to meet with you in person to discuss this matter further and provide you with the documents I have found. Please let me know if you are willing to meet, and I will make the necessary arrangements.

Thank you for your time and consideration.

Sincerely,

Lisa Bennett

Lisa hesitated for a moment before hitting send. She knew that once the email was sent, there would be no turning back. The decision weighed heavily on her, but she felt a sense of resolve. She had to do what was right, no matter the cost.

The next few days were a blur of anxiety and anticipation. Lisa continued to go to work, trying to maintain a semblance of normalcy while she waited for Jake's response. Every time her phone buzzed with a new email or message, her heart skipped a beat.

Finally, an email from Jake appeared in her inbox. Lisa's hands shook as she opened it. The message was brief but reassuring. Jake had agreed to meet her and had suggested a discreet location—a small café on the outskirts of the city. He assured her that he would take all necessary precautions to ensure their meeting was secure.

On the day of the meeting, Lisa dressed in a simple blouse and jeans, hoping to blend in and avoid drawing attention to herself. She arrived at the café early, choosing a table near the back where they would have some privacy. As she waited, she sipped on a cup of herbal tea, her nerves on edge.

A few minutes later, Jake walked in. He was taller than she had expected, with a rugged demeanor and a piercing gaze that seemed to see right through her. He wore a casual jacket and jeans, looking every bit the seasoned journalist he was.

"Lisa?" he asked, approaching her table.

"Yes," she replied, standing to shake his hand. "Thank you for meeting with me."

Jake nodded and took a seat across from her. "I read your email. It sounds like you've uncovered something significant. Can you tell me more about what you found?"

Lisa took a deep breath and began to recount her discovery, explaining the discrepancies in the expense reports and the suspicious transactions she had uncovered. She handed over copies of the documents she had brought with her, watching as Jake examined them with a practiced eye.

"This is damning evidence," Jake said, his tone serious. "If what you're saying is true, this could be one of the biggest corruption scandals in recent history. But we need to be careful. The people involved in this are powerful and won't hesitate to retaliate."

Lisa nodded, her heart pounding. "I know the risks, but I can't just ignore what I found. I need your help to expose this and protect myself."

Jake leaned back in his chair, considering her words. "I'll help you, but we need to proceed cautiously. I'll start by verifying the documents and gathering additional evidence. We'll need to build an airtight case before we go public. In the meantime, you need to be very careful. Don't talk about this with anyone at work, and take steps to protect your digital footprint."

Lisa agreed, feeling a mix of relief and trepidation. She knew that the road ahead would be difficult, but she also knew that she had made the right decision. With Jake's help, she would expose the corruption and hold those responsible accountable.

Over the next few weeks, Jake and his team worked tirelessly to investigate the corruption scheme. They dug deeper into the financial records, interviewed potential whistleblowers, and followed the money trail to its source. Lisa continued to provide them with information, discreetly passing along documents and insights while maintaining her cover at work.

As the investigation progressed, Lisa's anxiety grew. She felt like she was constantly looking over her shoulder, fearing that someone would discover what she was doing. She took extra precautions, using encrypted communication methods and avoiding any behavior that might raise suspicion.

Despite the stress and fear, Lisa found solace in her growing partnership with Jake. He was a steady presence, offering reassurance and guidance as they navigated the complexities of the investigation. They developed a deep trust and camaraderie, united by their shared commitment to exposing the truth.

One evening, as Lisa was leaving work, she noticed a black SUV parked across the street. It was the same vehicle she had seen several times over the past few days. Her heart raced as she realized she was being followed. She quickly changed her route, taking a circuitous path to shake off her pursuers.

When she arrived home, Lisa locked the door behind her and took a moment to collect herself. She knew that the danger was real and that she needed to stay vigilant. She contacted Jake, informing him of the situation.

"We need to escalate our security measures," Jake said, his voice tense. "I'll arrange for someone to keep an eye on your house and make sure you're not followed. We can't afford to take any chances."

Lisa agreed, grateful for Jake's support. The stakes were higher than ever, but she was determined to see this through. She knew that the truth had to come out, no matter the cost.

As the weeks turned into months, the investigation continued to gain momentum. Jake's team uncovered more evidence, linking the corruption scheme to high-ranking government officials and corporate executives. The scope of the scandal was staggering, involving millions of dollars in fraudulent contracts and kickbacks.

Lisa's role as a whistleblower became increasingly precarious. She continued to work at Meridian, maintaining her cover and providing Jake with valuable information. She felt a constant sense of tension, knowing that at any moment, her secret could be discovered.

One evening, as Lisa was preparing to leave work, she received a call from Jake. "We have enough evidence to go public," he said. "But we need to plan our next steps carefully. Once we publish the story, there will be a backlash, and we need to be prepared."

Lisa took a deep breath, feeling a mix of relief and apprehension. "I'm ready. Let's do this."

Jake outlined their plan, detailing how they would release the information and ensure Lisa's safety. They would publish a series of articles, gradually revealing the extent of the corruption and the identities of those involved. Jake's team would work closely with law enforcement to secure warrants and arrests, ensuring that the culprits faced justice.

The day of the first publication arrived. Lisa sat at her desk, her heart pounding as she watched the clock. She knew that once the article was released, there would be no turning back. She took a deep breath and braced herself for the storm that was about to come.

At exactly noon, Jake published the first article. The headline was bold and damning, exposing the corruption scheme and implicating high-ranking officials and corporate executives. The article included excerpts from the documents Lisa had uncovered, as well as testimonies from other whistleblowers who had come forward.

The reaction was immediate and explosive. News outlets across the country picked up the story, and social media was abuzz with outrage and calls for accountability. The public demanded answers, and pressure mounted on the government and Meridian Technologies to respond.

Lisa watched the unfolding drama with a mix of satisfaction and fear. She knew that the truth was finally out, but she also knew that the backlash would be swift and severe. She received a call from Jake, who reassured her that they were taking all necessary precautions to protect her.

"Stay strong, Lisa," Jake said. "We're in this together. The truth is out, and there's no stopping it now."

As the days passed, the fallout from the publication continued to escalate. Government officials and corporate executives issued denials and attempted to discredit the investigation, but the evidence was overwhelming. Law enforcement agencies launched investigations, and several high-profile arrests were made.

Lisa's life was turned upside down. She was placed under protective custody, and her movements were closely monitored to ensure her safety. She felt a mix of relief and anxiety, knowing that her actions had made a significant impact but also fearing the repercussions.

The media frenzy showed no signs of abating. Jake's team continued to publish articles, each one revealing more damning evidence and further implicating the corrupt network. The public's demand for justice grew louder, and the pressure on the government and Meridian Technologies intensified.

One evening, as Lisa was watching the news, she received a call from Jake. "We've done it," he said, his voice filled with triumph. "The corruption network is collapsing, and the people responsible are being brought to justice. Your bravery and determination have made all the difference."

Lisa felt a wave of emotion wash over her. She had risked everything to expose the truth, and now, her efforts were paying off. The corrupt officials and executives who had abused their power were being held accountable, and a sense of justice was beginning to prevail.

As the weeks turned into months, the investigation continued to yield results. More arrests were made, and additional whistleblowers came forward, bolstered by Lisa's example. The government enacted new regulations to prevent future corruption, and Meridian Technologies faced significant consequences for its role in the scandal.

Lisa's life gradually began to return to a semblance of normalcy. She continued to work closely with Jake and his team, providing support and guidance to other whistleblowers. She found solace in the knowledge that she had made a difference and helped to bring about positive change.

One evening, as Lisa sat in her living room, she received a call from her parents. They had seen the news and were proud of her bravery and determination. Her younger brother, who had always looked up to her, expressed his admiration for her courage.

"We're so proud of you, Lisa," her mother said, her voice filled with emotion. "You've done something incredible, and we're here to support you every step of the way."

Lisa felt a sense of gratitude and relief. She had feared that her actions would alienate her from her family, but instead, they had brought them closer together. She knew that she had made the right decision, and she was ready to face whatever challenges lay ahead.

As she looked out at the city skyline, Lisa felt a renewed sense of purpose. The journey had been long and difficult, but she had emerged stronger and more determined than ever. She knew that the fight for justice was far from over, but she was ready to continue the battle, knowing that the truth had the power to change the world.

With Jake and her newfound allies by her side, Lisa embarked on the next chapter of her life. She was no longer just a mid-level employee at a government contractor—she was a symbol of courage and integrity, a whistleblower who had stood up against corruption and helped to bring about a new era of transparency and accountability. The road ahead was uncertain, but Lisa was ready to face it head-on, knowing that her actions had made a lasting impact and inspired others to do the same.

# Chapter 3: The Investigation

The days after the initial meeting between Lisa Bennett and Jake Harrison were a whirlwind of intense activity and careful strategizing. Lisa had taken a monumental step in bringing the corruption at Meridian Technologies to light, and now, the real work began. Jake and his team knew they needed to dig deep and gather as much evidence as possible to build an irrefutable case. This chapter details the rigorous investigation that followed and the critical alliances formed along the way.

## Deep Dive

JAKE HARRISON SAT IN his cluttered office, a makeshift war room filled with stacks of papers, computer monitors, and a whiteboard covered in scribbles and diagrams. The atmosphere was charged with urgency and determination as Jake and his team pored over the documents Lisa had provided. The evidence was damning, but they needed more. They needed to corroborate every detail, cross-reference every figure, and build a comprehensive narrative that would withstand the scrutiny of public opinion and the courts.

"Okay, team," Jake began, addressing his assembled colleagues. "We have a lot to cover. Lisa's documents give us a solid starting point, but we need to dig deeper. We need to follow the money trail, identify key players, and uncover any additional evidence that ties everything together. Let's get to work."

The team members nodded, their faces set with resolve. There was Sarah, a data analyst with a knack for uncovering hidden patterns; Mark, a seasoned investigator with a background in law enforcement; and Emily, a journalist known for her relentless pursuit of the truth. Together, they formed a formidable force, each bringing their unique skills to the table.

Sarah began by digitizing the documents and entering the data into a secure database. She meticulously cross-referenced the information with public records, financial statements, and other sources. Her goal was to identify discrepancies, trace the flow of funds, and uncover connections that might not be immediately apparent.

"Jake, take a look at this," Sarah called out, gesturing to her screen. "I've found several payments to a company called Triton Solutions. The amounts are significant, but I can't find any legitimate business dealings or services provided by this company. It looks like a shell corporation."

Jake leaned over to examine the data. "Good catch, Sarah. Let's see if we can find out who owns Triton Solutions and where the money is going. This could be a key piece of the puzzle."

Meanwhile, Mark was tasked with tracking down potential witnesses and informants. He reached out to former employees of Meridian Technologies, contractors, and anyone who might have knowledge of the corrupt activities. Mark's background in law enforcement gave him a unique perspective and the skills needed to persuade reluctant individuals to come forward.

One afternoon, Mark received a promising lead. He had been in contact with a former accountant at Meridian, a woman named Karen, who had left the company under mysterious circumstances. After several phone calls and assurances of confidentiality, Karen agreed to meet in person.

"Thank you for meeting with me, Karen," Mark said as they sat down in a quiet café. "I understand this must be difficult, but your information could be crucial in exposing the corruption at Meridian Technologies."

Karen nodded, her expression tense but determined. "I left Meridian because I couldn't stand what was happening there. I saw things—fraudulent transactions, kickbacks, payments to offshore accounts. I tried to speak up, but I was silenced and pushed out. I have records that I took with me. I was afraid to come forward, but if it means stopping this corruption, I'll help."

Mark smiled reassuringly. "You're doing the right thing, Karen. We will protect your identity and make sure your information is used to bring these people to justice."

While Sarah and Mark focused on their respective tasks, Emily delved into the backgrounds of the key figures implicated in the documents. She tracked down their professional histories, affiliations, and any public records that might shed light on their activities. Emily's investigative skills and network of sources allowed her to uncover connections and patterns that others might miss.

One evening, as the team gathered to review their progress, Emily shared her findings. "I've been looking into the executives at Meridian and the government officials mentioned in the documents. There are some interesting connections. For instance, several of these officials have received campaign contributions and favors from companies tied to the shell corporations Sarah identified. It's a classic quid pro quo."

Jake nodded thoughtfully. "Great work, Emily. This is exactly what we need to build our case. Now, let's see if we can find more direct evidence—emails, memos, anything that explicitly shows their involvement in the corruption."

# Gathering Allies

AS THE INVESTIGATION progressed, Lisa continued to play a crucial role. Despite the risk, she discreetly reached out to colleagues within Meridian Technologies who might be willing to come forward with additional information. She knew that the more evidence they could gather, the stronger their case would be.

One of the first people Lisa approached was Tom, an IT specialist she had worked with for years. Tom was known for his integrity and had often expressed frustration with the company's questionable practices. Lisa arranged to meet him at a local park, away from the prying eyes of Meridian's security.

"Tom, I need to talk to you about something important," Lisa began, her voice low and urgent. "I've discovered evidence of massive corruption at Meridian, and I'm working with an investigative journalist to expose it. We need your help. Do you have access to any internal communications or records that could support our case?"

Tom looked around nervously before responding. "Lisa, I knew something was wrong, but I never imagined it was this big. I can access the email servers and internal databases. I'll see what I can find, but we need to be careful. If they catch wind of this, we could both be in serious trouble."

Lisa nodded. "I understand the risks, but we have to do what's right. Please, Tom, anything you can find will make a difference."

Over the next few days, Tom covertly accessed Meridian's email servers and databases, copying relevant communications and records. He managed to find several emails that explicitly discussed the fraudulent transactions and payments to shell corporations. The emails included conversations between high-ranking executives and government officials, outlining their schemes and attempts to cover their tracks.

Tom provided the information to Lisa, who then passed it on to Jake and his team. The new evidence was a goldmine, providing direct proof of the corruption and implicating key players in the scandal.

In addition to Tom, Lisa reached out to other potential allies within the company. She carefully chose individuals she believed shared her sense of integrity and justice. One of these individuals was Maria, a senior project manager who had always been vocal about ethical practices and transparency.

"Maria, I need to talk to you about something serious," Lisa said, arranging to meet her at a quiet café. "I've uncovered evidence of corruption at Meridian, and I'm working with an investigative journalist to expose it. We need your help. Do you have any information or records that could support our case?"

Maria's eyes widened in shock. "Lisa, I've suspected for a long time that something was wrong, but I never had concrete proof. I have access to project files and financial records. I'll see what I can find, but we need to be extremely careful. If they find out we're involved, they won't hesitate to retaliate."

Lisa nodded. "I know the risks, but we have to do what's right. Please, Maria, anything you can find will help bring these people to justice."

Maria began discreetly reviewing project files and financial records, looking for any discrepancies or evidence of fraudulent activities. She managed to find several documents that detailed inflated project costs, kickbacks, and payments to contractors with no legitimate work history. Maria provided the information to Lisa, who then passed it on to Jake and his team.

As the investigation continued, Lisa and Jake's team worked tirelessly to compile and corroborate the evidence. They knew that building an airtight case was crucial, and they left no stone unturned in their pursuit of the truth.

# The Breakthrough

ONE EVENING, AS THE team gathered to review their progress, Jake received a call from an anonymous source. The caller claimed to have information that could blow the case wide open but insisted on meeting in person. Jake agreed to the meeting, knowing that it could be a game-changer.

The meeting took place in a dimly lit parking garage, adding to the air of intrigue and danger. The source, a former high-level executive at Meridian who had fallen out of favor with the corrupt network, provided Jake with a USB drive containing explosive evidence.

"These files contain detailed records of the corruption scheme," the source explained. "They include emails, financial transactions, and internal memos that explicitly outline the illegal activities. This is everything you need to take them down."

Jake thanked the source and returned to the office, eager to review the new evidence. As he and his team examined the files, they realized that they had struck gold. The documents provided a comprehensive account of the corruption, including the names of all key players, the methods they used to launder money, and their attempts to cover their tracks.

"This is it," Jake said, his voice filled with excitement. "This is the smoking gun we've been looking for. With this evidence, we can build an irrefutable case and bring these people to justice."

# The Final Steps

WITH THE NEW EVIDENCE in hand, Jake and his team worked tirelessly to finalize their investigation. They cross-referenced the information with the documents Lisa and her allies had provided, ensuring that every detail was corroborated and verified. The team knew that they had to be meticulous, as any discrepancy or error could be used to discredit their work.

Lisa continued to play a crucial role, providing additional information and support as needed. She also remained in contact with the other whistleblowers, offering reassurance and guidance as they navigated the risks and challenges of their involvement.

One evening, as Lisa sat in her apartment, she received a call from Jake. "We're ready," he said. "We have everything we need to go public. But we need to plan our next steps carefully. Once we release this information, there will be a backlash, and we need to be prepared."

Lisa took a deep breath, feeling a mix of relief and apprehension. "I'm ready. Let's do this."

Jake outlined their plan, detailing how they would release the information and ensure everyone's safety. They would publish a series of articles, gradually revealing the extent of the corruption and the identities of those involved. Jake's team would work closely with law enforcement to secure warrants and arrests, ensuring that the culprits faced justice.

The day of the first publication arrived. Lisa sat at her desk, her heart pounding as she watched the clock. She knew that once the article was released, there would be no turning back. She took a deep breath and braced herself for the storm that was about to come.

At exactly noon, Jake published the first article. The headline was bold and damning, exposing the corruption scheme and implicating high-ranking officials and corporate executives. The article included excerpts from the documents Lisa had uncovered, as well as testimonies from other whistleblowers who had come forward.

The reaction was immediate and explosive. News outlets across the country picked up the story, and social media was abuzz with outrage and calls for accountability. The public demanded answers, and pressure mounted on the government and Meridian Technologies to respond.

Lisa watched the unfolding drama with a mix of satisfaction and fear. She knew that the truth was finally out, but she also knew that the backlash would be swift and severe. She received a call from Jake, who reassured her that they were taking all necessary precautions to protect her.

"Stay strong, Lisa," Jake said. "We're in this together. The truth is out, and there's no stopping it now."

As the days passed, the fallout from the publication continued to escalate. Government officials and corporate executives issued denials and attempted to discredit the investigation, but the evidence was overwhelming. Law enforcement agencies launched investigations, and several high-profile arrests were made.

Lisa's life was turned upside down. She was placed under protective custody, and her movements were closely monitored to ensure her safety. She felt a mix of relief and anxiety, knowing that her actions had made a significant impact but also fearing the repercussions.

The media frenzy showed no signs of abating. Jake's team continued to publish articles, each one revealing more damning evidence and further implicating the corrupt network. The public's demand for justice grew louder, and the pressure on the government and Meridian Technologies intensified.

One evening, as Lisa was watching the news, she received a call from Jake. "We've done it," he said, his voice filled with triumph. "The corruption network is collapsing, and the people responsible are being brought to justice. Your bravery and determination have made all the difference."

Lisa felt a wave of emotion wash over her. She had risked everything to expose the truth, and now, her efforts were paying off. The corrupt officials and executives who had abused their power were being held accountable, and a sense of justice was beginning to prevail.

As the weeks turned into months, the investigation continued to yield results. More arrests were made, and additional whistleblowers came forward, bolstered by Lisa's example. The government enacted new regulations to prevent future corruption, and Meridian Technologies faced significant consequences for its role in the scandal.

Lisa's life gradually began to return to a semblance of normalcy. She continued to work closely with Jake and his team, providing support and guidance to other whistleblowers. She found solace in the knowledge that she had made a difference and helped to bring about positive change.

One evening, as Lisa sat in her living room, she received a call from her parents. They had seen the news and were proud of her bravery and determination. Her younger brother, who had always looked up to her, expressed his admiration for her courage.

"We're so proud of you, Lisa," her mother said, her voice filled with emotion. "You've done something incredible, and we're here to support you every step of the way."

Lisa felt a sense of gratitude and relief. She had feared that her actions would alienate her from her family, but instead, they had brought them closer together. She knew that she had made the right decision, and she was ready to face whatever challenges lay ahead.

As she looked out at the city skyline, Lisa felt a renewed sense of purpose. The journey had been long and difficult, but she had emerged stronger and more determined than ever. She knew that the fight for justice was far from over, but she was ready to continue the battle, knowing that the truth had the power to change the world.

With Jake and her newfound allies by her side, Lisa embarked on the next chapter of her life. She was no longer just a mid-level employee at a government contractor—she was a symbol of courage and integrity, a whistleblower who had stood up against corruption and helped to bring about a new era of transparency and accountability. The road ahead was uncertain, but Lisa was ready to face it head-on, knowing that her actions had made a lasting impact and inspired others to do the same.

# Chapter 4: The First Leak

The morning air was thick with anticipation. The first article detailing the corruption at Meridian Technologies was set to go live at noon. Jake Harrison and his team had worked tirelessly to prepare for this moment. Every fact had been double-checked, every source verified, and every potential backlash anticipated. As the hour approached, the tension in the newsroom was palpable.

Lisa Bennett, the whistleblower whose courage had set the entire investigation in motion, sat in a safe house provided by Jake's network of allies. She was under protective custody, far from her familiar surroundings at Meridian Technologies. The anxiety of waiting gnawed at her, but she knew this was necessary. Her identity had to remain a secret for now, for her safety and the integrity of the investigation.

Jake, with his characteristic focus and determination, gathered his team for a final briefing. "We're about to publish the first article. This is just the beginning. Remember, the goal is to expose the truth, piece by piece. We need to keep the pressure on and ensure that our work is irrefutable."

His team nodded, understanding the gravity of the situation. They had all sacrificed a great deal to get to this point, and they knew the risks involved. But they were united by a common purpose: to bring the truth to light and hold those responsible accountable.

At exactly noon, Jake pressed the button that published the article to the news website. The headline was bold and unambiguous:

## "Uncovering Corruption: Meridian Technologies and the Government's Dark Secret"

THE ARTICLE BEGAN WITH a detailed account of the fraudulent transactions and illicit payments that Lisa had discovered. It included excerpts from the documents she had provided, along with testimonies from other whistleblowers who had come forward. The article meticulously outlined the corruption scheme, implicating several high-ranking officials and corporate executives without revealing Lisa's identity.

As soon as the article went live, the response was immediate and explosive. News outlets across the country picked up the story, and social media erupted with outrage. The hashtag #MeridianCorruption began trending within minutes, as people expressed their shock and demanded accountability.

Within hours, the news reached the highest levels of government and the corporate world. The implicated officials and executives were quick to issue statements, vehemently denying the allegations and attempting to discredit the article.

"These accusations are completely unfounded," said Richard Collins, a senior executive at Meridian Technologies, in a hastily arranged press conference. "We operate with the highest standards of integrity and transparency. This is clearly an attempt to tarnish our reputation."

Government officials echoed similar sentiments. Senator John Mitchell, one of the officials named in the article, took to the airwaves to defend himself. "These are baseless accusations with no merit. I have always served the public with honesty and dedication. This is nothing more than a smear campaign."

Despite their denials, the public was not convinced. The evidence presented in the article was compelling, and the level of detail made it clear that this was not a simple misunderstanding or a smear. The public uproar grew louder, with calls for independent investigations and accountability.

Jake's phone rang incessantly as journalists, news anchors, and public figures sought interviews and comments. He maintained his composure, giving carefully measured responses and emphasizing the importance of transparency and accountability.

"We have presented irrefutable evidence of corruption," Jake said in an interview with a major news network. "Our investigation is ongoing, and we will continue to release more information in the coming days. The public deserves to know the truth, and those responsible must be held accountable."

Back at the safe house, Lisa watched the news coverage with a mix of relief and anxiety. The truth was finally out, but she knew this was just the beginning. The initial denials and damage control were expected, but she feared what might come next. The people she had exposed were powerful and would not go down without a fight.

Later that evening, Jake convened a meeting with his team to assess the situation and plan their next steps. The room was filled with a sense of urgency and determination.

"We've made a strong impact with the first article," Jake began. "But we need to keep up the momentum. Our next article will delve deeper into the financial transactions and provide more concrete evidence. We also need to be prepared for their counterattacks. They're going to come after us hard."

Sarah, the data analyst, nodded in agreement. "I've been cross-referencing the financial records we obtained from Lisa and the other whistleblowers. There's a clear pattern of money laundering and kickbacks. We need to make this information public as soon as possible."

Mark, the seasoned investigator, added, "I've been in contact with several more potential witnesses. Some of them are scared, but they're willing to come forward if we can guarantee their safety. Their testimonies will be crucial in building our case."

Emily, the relentless journalist, chimed in. "I'll work on gathering more background information on the key figures involved. We need to paint a complete picture of their corruption and how deep it goes."

Jake looked around the room at his dedicated team. "Excellent. Let's get to work. The truth is on our side, and we won't stop until justice is served."

As the team dispersed to their tasks, Lisa felt a sense of solidarity and purpose. She had taken a huge risk in coming forward, but she was not alone in this fight. With Jake and his team by her side, she felt a renewed determination to see this through to the end.

Over the next few days, Jake's team worked tirelessly to prepare the next article. They pored over financial records, interviewed witnesses, and gathered more evidence. The pressure was mounting, and they knew that the stakes were higher than ever.

Meanwhile, the implicated officials and executives intensified their efforts to discredit the investigation. They hired high-powered public relations firms, launched legal threats, and spread misinformation in an attempt to muddy the waters and cast doubt on the validity of the accusations.

Despite these efforts, the public's demand for accountability grew louder. Protests erupted outside Meridian Technologies' headquarters and government buildings, with people carrying signs that read "Justice for the People" and "End Corruption Now." The pressure on the authorities to take action was immense.

As the second article went live, it provided even more damning evidence of the corruption scheme. It included detailed financial records, emails, and internal memos that explicitly showed the involvement of the implicated officials and executives. The article also featured testimonies from former employees and whistleblowers who corroborated the findings.

The fallout from the second article was immediate. Several high-ranking officials and corporate executives were placed under investigation, and calls for their resignations grew louder. The public's trust in the government and Meridian Technologies continued to erode, and the demand for justice reached a fever pitch.

Jake and his team received numerous threats and attempts to intimidate them into silence. But they remained undeterred, knowing that they were on the right side of history. They continued to gather evidence, prepare more articles, and work closely with law enforcement to ensure that the truth would prevail.

As the investigation progressed, Lisa's role as a whistleblower became even more critical. She continued to provide valuable information and support to Jake's team, knowing that her actions were making a difference. The risk was great, but the cause was greater.

One evening, as Lisa sat in the safe house, she received a call from Jake. "We're making progress," he said. "The authorities are finally taking action, and several key players are facing charges. But we can't let our guard down. They're still trying to fight back."

Lisa nodded, feeling a mix of relief and resolve. "I understand, Jake. I'm in this for the long haul. Whatever it takes to bring them to justice."

As the weeks turned into months, the investigation continued to yield results. More articles were published, each one revealing new layers of corruption and further implicating the key figures involved. The public's demand for accountability remained strong, and the authorities were forced to take decisive action.

Several high-profile arrests were made, and the implicated officials and executives faced legal battles that would likely end their careers. The government enacted new regulations and oversight mechanisms to prevent future corruption, and Meridian Technologies faced significant consequences for its role in the scandal.

Lisa's life gradually began to return to a semblance of normalcy. She continued to work closely with Jake and his team, providing support and guidance to other whistleblowers. She found solace in the knowledge that she had made a difference and helped to bring about positive change.

One evening, as Lisa sat in her living room, she received a call from her parents. They had seen the news and were proud of her bravery and determination. Her younger brother, who had always looked up to her, expressed his admiration for her courage.

"We're so proud of you, Lisa," her mother said, her voice filled with emotion. "You've done something incredible, and we're here to support you every step of the way."

Lisa felt a sense of gratitude and relief. She had feared that her actions would alienate her from her family, but instead, they had brought them closer together. She knew that she had made the right decision, and she was ready to face whatever challenges lay ahead.

As she looked out at the city skyline, Lisa felt a renewed sense of purpose. The journey had been long and difficult, but she had emerged stronger and more determined than ever. She knew that the fight for justice was far from over, but she was ready to continue the battle, knowing that the truth had the power to change the world.

With Jake and her newfound allies by her side, Lisa embarked on the next chapter of her life. She was no longer just a mid-level employee at a government contractor—she was a symbol of courage and integrity, a whistleblower who had stood up against corruption and helped to bring about a new era of transparency and accountability. The road ahead was uncertain, but Lisa was ready to face it head-on, knowing that her actions had made a lasting impact and inspired others to do the same.

# Chapter 5: The Backlash

The initial shockwaves from Jake Harrison's explosive investigation into Meridian Technologies and the implicated government officials had settled into a tense, watchful quiet. For Jake and his team, the days following the first and second articles had been a whirlwind of media attention, public support, and heightened security measures. The public's demand for accountability was a force that could not be ignored, but the backlash from the powerful entities they had exposed was brewing just beneath the surface.

## Retaliation Begins

IN THE QUIET OF HIS office, Jake Harrison reviewed the latest updates from his team. The investigation was progressing steadily, and they were uncovering more damning evidence with each passing day. Yet, the tension was palpable. The walls seemed to close in, and Jake could almost feel the eyes of those he had exposed watching his every move.

It began with the legal threats. Jake's phone buzzed with a new email, and as he opened it, he saw the letterhead of one of the most prestigious law firms in the country. The message was clear: a cease and desist order demanding that he halt all publications related to Meridian Technologies and the implicated officials. The letter threatened a defamation lawsuit that could potentially bankrupt him and his publication.

Jake forwarded the email to his lawyer, Sarah, who had been an invaluable ally throughout this ordeal. Moments later, his phone rang.

"Jake, I've read the letter," Sarah said, her voice steady. "It's a scare tactic. They're trying to intimidate you into silence. We expected this. I'm preparing a response. We have the truth on our side, and their threats won't hold up in court."

Jake sighed, running a hand through his hair. "Thanks, Sarah. I knew they wouldn't take this lying down, but it's still unnerving. How's the team holding up?"

Sarah paused. "They're feeling the pressure, but they're committed. We all are. Stay strong, Jake. We're in this together."

As the legal threats mounted, Jake's team also began experiencing other forms of harassment. Their offices were subject to random inspections by city officials, likely orchestrated by those trying to undermine their work. Anonymous calls and emails flooded their inboxes, questioning their credibility and attempting to discredit their findings.

One evening, as Jake was leaving the office, he noticed a car parked across the street with two men inside. The same car had been there the night before. He took a mental note of the license plate and made a call to Mark, the seasoned investigator on his team.

"Mark, I think I'm being followed," Jake said, his voice low and cautious. "There's a car parked outside. I've seen it a few times now."

Mark's voice was calm but serious. "I'll look into it, Jake. In the meantime, be careful. These people won't hesitate to use intimidation tactics."

Jake nodded, feeling the weight of the situation pressing down on him. The corrupt entities they had exposed were powerful and had resources at their disposal that Jake's team could scarcely imagine.

## Lisa's Fears Realized

MEANWHILE, LISA BENNETT, the whistleblower whose bravery had set the investigation in motion, was also feeling the heat. She had been relocated to a safe house, but the sense of safety it provided was fragile. Every creak of the floorboards, every shadow outside the window made her jump. She knew that the people she had exposed would stop at nothing to silence her.

One morning, Lisa received an anonymous package at the safe house. Inside was a single sheet of paper with a chilling message: "We know where you are. Stay quiet, or else."

Her hands trembled as she read the words. She called Jake immediately, her voice shaking. "Jake, I got a threat. They know where I am."

Jake's heart sank. "Stay calm, Lisa. We're increasing security measures around the safe house. I'll have Mark and his team look into this. You're not alone."

But the threats didn't stop there. Lisa's phone rang incessantly with unknown numbers, and when she answered, she was met with silence or sinister laughter. Her social media accounts were hacked, and false information about her was spread online, painting her as a disgruntled employee seeking revenge.

The harassment took a toll on Lisa's mental health. She found it increasingly difficult to sleep, her nights plagued by nightmares of being pursued and silenced. Her waking hours were filled with anxiety, and she began to second-guess her decision to come forward. Had she made a mistake? Was it worth the risk?

One evening, as Lisa sat in the dimly lit living room of the safe house, she received a call from her parents. Their voices were filled with concern, having seen the news and the online attacks against her.

"Lisa, are you okay?" her mother asked, her voice trembling. "We're worried about you. Maybe it's not too late to back out."

Tears welled up in Lisa's eyes. "I don't know, Mom. I thought I was doing the right thing, but now... I don't know if I can handle this."

Her father spoke up, his tone gentle but firm. "Lisa, you've always been strong. You've done something incredibly brave. Don't let them scare you into silence. We're here for you, no matter what."

The conversation with her parents gave Lisa a glimmer of hope, but the fear remained. She knew that backing out now would not only mean giving up on the fight for justice but also putting herself at greater risk. She had come too far to turn back.

## The Team's Resolve

BACK AT THE OFFICE, Jake and his team convened a meeting to discuss the escalating threats and plan their next steps. The room was filled with a sense of urgency and determination.

"We're all feeling the pressure," Jake began, looking around at his team. "But we can't let them intimidate us into silence. The public is counting on us to expose the truth. We need to stay focused and vigilant."

Sarah, the data analyst, spoke up. "I've been receiving anonymous emails trying to discredit my work. They're saying that our data is flawed and that we're making baseless accusations."

Mark, the seasoned investigator, added, "I've been followed, and my phone has been tapped. They're trying to find any weak spot they can exploit."

Emily, the journalist, nodded. "I've been harassed online and received threats. But we can't let them scare us. We have the evidence, and we need to keep pushing forward."

Jake listened to his team, feeling a mix of pride and concern. "We knew this would be dangerous, but we're doing the right thing. Let's tighten our security measures and continue to support each other. We're in this together."

The team agreed, their resolve strengthened by the solidarity they felt. They knew that the fight for justice would not be easy, but they were committed to seeing it through.

## Escalating Threats

THE HARASSMENT AND intimidation tactics escalated in the days that followed. Jake received a call from his lawyer, Sarah, with alarming news.

"Jake, they've filed a defamation lawsuit against you and the publication," Sarah said. "They're claiming that we've made false accusations and damaged their reputations. It's a strategic lawsuit intended to silence us."

Jake felt a surge of anger. "They think they can scare us into backing down. But we're not going to stop. What are our options?"

Sarah sighed. "We'll fight the lawsuit, but it's going to be a long and expensive battle. We'll need to raise funds for legal fees and prepare for a protracted fight."

Jake nodded, determination in his eyes. "We'll do whatever it takes. The truth is worth fighting for."

Meanwhile, Lisa's situation continued to deteriorate. The harassment intensified, with unknown callers making threats against her family. Her parents received ominous messages, and her younger brother was followed home from school. The fear that gripped Lisa's heart was overwhelming.

One night, as she sat alone in the safe house, the lights flickered, and the power went out. Lisa's heart raced as she heard footsteps outside the door. She grabbed her phone and called Jake, her voice shaking.

"Jake, someone's here. The power's out, and I can hear footsteps outside."

"Stay calm, Lisa," Jake replied, his voice steady. "I'm sending security over right now. Lock all the doors and stay away from the windows."

Minutes felt like hours as Lisa waited in the dark, her breath coming in short, panicked bursts. She heard the sound of a car approaching and then voices outside. The security team Jake had sent arrived and quickly assessed the situation.

"It's okay, Lisa. We're here," one of the security personnel said as they entered the safe house. "We'll stay with you and make sure you're safe."

The incident left Lisa shaken, but it also solidified her resolve. She knew that the threats were meant to break her, to make her question her decision and give up. But she couldn't let fear dictate her actions. She had come too far and sacrificed too much to turn back now.

# Fighting Back

DESPITE THE ESCALATING threats and harassment, Jake and his team continued their investigation with renewed determination. They knew that the backlash was a sign that they were making an impact, that the powerful entities they had exposed were feeling the heat.

Jake decided to go public with the threats and harassment his team and Lisa were facing. He organized a press conference, inviting media outlets to cover the ongoing investigation and the retaliatory tactics being used against them.

Standing before a room filled with journalists and cameras, Jake began his statement. "In our pursuit of the truth, my team and I have faced significant harassment and intimidation. We've received legal threats, been followed, and had our credibility attacked. Our whistleblower, whose bravery brought this corruption to light, has faced even worse—threats to her life and her family."

He paused, letting his words sink in. "But we will not be silenced. We have the evidence, and we will continue to expose the truth. The public deserves to know what is happening behind closed doors, and we will not stop until justice is served."

The press conference generated significant media coverage, drawing public attention to the retaliatory tactics being used against Jake and his team. The public's support grew stronger, with many expressing their outrage at the attempts to silence those who were fighting for justice.

The increased visibility also brought additional support from other journalists, activists, and legal experts who offered their assistance. The team received donations to help cover legal fees, and several prominent figures publicly endorsed their efforts.

## A Turning Point

ONE EVENING, AS JAKE and his team reviewed their latest findings, they received a call from an unexpected source. A high-ranking official within the government, who had previously remained silent, offered to provide additional evidence and testify against the corrupt network.

"I've seen what you've been doing, and I can no longer stay silent," the official said, his voice filled with conviction. "I have documents and information that will further incriminate those involved. I'm willing to testify, but I need your protection."

Jake's heart raced with excitement. This could be the breakthrough they needed. "Thank you for coming forward. We'll do everything we can to protect you and ensure that your testimony is heard."

With the new evidence and the official's testimony, Jake and his team prepared their next article. They knew that this could be a turning point in their investigation, a chance to deliver a decisive blow to the corrupt network.

As the article went live, it revealed even more damning evidence of corruption and illegal activities. The official's testimony provided firsthand accounts of the schemes and the involvement of high-ranking officials. The public's reaction was immediate and explosive, with calls for resignations and further investigations.

The authorities could no longer ignore the mounting evidence. Several high-profile arrests were made, and the government launched an independent inquiry into the corruption scandal. The implicated officials and executives faced intense scrutiny, and their attempts to discredit the investigation fell flat.

# The Aftermath

THE INCREASED PRESSURE and public scrutiny began to take its toll on the corrupt network. As more evidence came to light, the web of deceit unraveled, and those involved faced the consequences of their actions.

For Jake and his team, the fight was far from over, but they had made significant progress. The public's support and the new evidence had given them the momentum they needed to continue their work.

Lisa, still under protective custody, watched the news with a mix of relief and resolve. The threats and harassment had not broken her spirit. Instead, they had strengthened her determination to see justice served.

One evening, as Lisa sat in the safe house, she received a call from Jake. "We've made significant progress, Lisa. The authorities are taking action, and the public is behind us. Your bravery has made a difference."

Lisa smiled, feeling a sense of hope. "Thank you, Jake. I couldn't have done this without you and the team. We're not done yet, but we're getting closer."

As the weeks turned into months, the investigation continued to yield results. More articles were published, each one revealing new layers of corruption and further implicating the key figures involved. The public's demand for accountability remained strong, and the authorities were forced to take decisive action.

Several high-profile arrests were made, and the implicated officials and executives faced legal battles that would likely end their careers. The government enacted new regulations and oversight mechanisms to prevent future corruption, and Meridian Technologies faced significant consequences for its role in the scandal.

Lisa's life gradually began to return to a semblance of normalcy. She continued to work closely with Jake and his team, providing support and guidance to other whistleblowers. She found solace in the knowledge that she had made a difference and helped to bring about positive change.

One evening, as Lisa sat in her living room, she received a call from her parents. They had seen the news and were proud of her bravery and determination. Her younger brother, who had always looked up to her, expressed his admiration for her courage.

"We're so proud of you, Lisa," her mother said, her voice filled with emotion. "You've done something incredible, and we're here to support you every step of the way."

Lisa felt a sense of gratitude and relief. She had feared that her actions would alienate her from her family, but instead, they had brought them closer together. She knew that she had made the right decision, and she was ready to face whatever challenges lay ahead.

As she looked out at the city skyline, Lisa felt a renewed sense of purpose. The journey had been long and difficult, but she had emerged stronger and more determined than ever. She knew that the fight for justice was far from over, but she was ready to continue the battle, knowing that the truth had the power to change the world.

With Jake and her newfound allies by her side, Lisa embarked on the next chapter of her life. She was no longer just a mid-level employee at a government contractor—she was a symbol of courage and integrity, a whistleblower who had stood up against corruption and helped to bring about a new era of transparency and accountability. The road ahead was uncertain, but Lisa was ready to face it head-on, knowing that her actions had made a lasting impact and inspired others to do the same.

# Chapter 6: The Support Network

The initial wave of public outrage following the publication of Jake Harrison's articles had subsided into a tense anticipation of what was to come. Lisa Bennett, the courageous whistleblower, had endured weeks of relentless harassment and intimidation. Despite the escalating threats, Lisa knew she had to stay the course. The truth had to be revealed, and those responsible for the corruption had to be held accountable. But she couldn't do it alone.

## Finding Allies

ONE EVENING, AS LISA sat in the safe house provided by Jake's network, her phone buzzed with a message from Jake. He had arranged a meeting with a group of whistleblower advocates and legal experts who could offer protection and support. Lisa felt a mix of relief and apprehension. She knew she needed help, but the thought of meeting new people and sharing her story once again filled her with anxiety.

Jake had chosen a discreet location for the meeting—a private conference room in a nondescript office building. As Lisa arrived, she was greeted by a friendly receptionist who escorted her to the room. Inside, she found Jake and a small group of individuals seated around a table. Each person exuded a sense of purpose and resolve.

"Lisa, I'd like you to meet some of our allies," Jake said, standing to introduce her. "This is Dr. Karen Mitchell, a psychologist specializing in trauma and whistleblower support; Tom Reynolds, a former prosecutor turned whistleblower advocate; and Sarah Hayes, a legal expert with years of experience in whistleblower protection."

Each person greeted Lisa warmly, making her feel instantly welcome. Despite their different backgrounds, they shared a common goal: to support and protect whistleblowers like Lisa.

"Thank you all for being here," Lisa said, taking a seat. "I appreciate your help. This has been a difficult journey, and I know I can't do it alone."

Dr. Mitchell, a compassionate woman with kind eyes, spoke first. "Lisa, you're incredibly brave for coming forward. The challenges you're facing are daunting, but you're not alone. We're here to support you in any way we can."

Tom Reynolds, a stern but empathetic man, added, "I've seen firsthand how powerful entities can retaliate against whistleblowers. But I've also seen the difference that a strong support network can make. We're going to ensure you have the protection you need and the resources to continue your fight."

Sarah Hayes, with her sharp legal mind, offered reassurance. "Legally, we have several options to protect you and hold those responsible accountable. We'll guide you through the process and ensure that your rights are upheld."

The meeting continued with a detailed discussion of the support they could offer. Dr. Mitchell would provide counseling and psychological support to help Lisa cope with the stress and trauma she was experiencing. Tom would coordinate protection measures and liaise with law enforcement to ensure her safety. Sarah would handle the legal aspects, from filing protective orders to preparing for potential court battles.

As the evening progressed, Lisa felt a growing sense of relief. The network of allies Jake had assembled was formidable, and their collective expertise gave her a renewed sense of hope. For the first time in weeks, she felt that she was no longer fighting this battle alone.

## Strengthening Resolve

OVER THE FOLLOWING days, Lisa began working closely with her new support network. Dr. Mitchell provided regular counseling sessions, helping Lisa process her emotions and develop coping strategies. The sessions were a safe space where Lisa could express her fears, frustrations, and hopes.

"You're doing remarkably well, Lisa," Dr. Mitchell said during one session. "It's natural to feel overwhelmed, but remember that your actions are making a significant impact. You're a catalyst for change."

Lisa nodded, feeling a sense of validation. "It's hard sometimes, but knowing that I'm making a difference keeps me going."

Tom Reynolds, meanwhile, had arranged for increased security around the safe house. He had also set up secure communication channels to ensure that Lisa could stay in touch with Jake and the team without fear of being monitored.

"Your safety is our top priority," Tom told her. "We've taken all necessary precautions, but always stay vigilant. If anything seems off, contact me immediately."

Lisa appreciated Tom's straightforward approach. His experience as a prosecutor gave him a unique perspective on the dangers she faced, and his no-nonsense attitude provided a sense of reassurance.

Sarah Hayes began preparing the legal groundwork for the upcoming battles. She reviewed all the evidence collected so far, cross-referencing it with legal statutes and precedents. Sarah's meticulous attention to detail and deep understanding of the law were invaluable.

"Legally, we have a strong case," Sarah explained during one of their meetings. "But we need to be prepared for a long fight. The entities we're up against have significant resources. However, with the evidence we've gathered and the public support we've garnered, we have a real chance of holding them accountable."

With the support of this network, Lisa felt her resolve strengthening. She was no longer consumed by fear and doubt. Instead, she felt empowered by the collective expertise and dedication of those around her. Every day, her determination to see justice served grew stronger.

One evening, as Lisa and Jake reviewed the latest developments in the case, Jake shared some encouraging news. "We've received offers of support from several prominent figures in the whistleblower community. They're willing to lend their voices to our cause and help amplify our message."

Lisa felt a surge of hope. "That's amazing, Jake. The more support we have, the harder it will be for them to silence us."

Jake nodded. "Exactly. We're building a movement, Lisa. Your courage has inspired others, and together, we're going to make a difference."

As the days turned into weeks, the investigation continued to gain momentum. Jake and his team published more articles, each one revealing new layers of corruption and further implicating the key figures involved. The public's demand for accountability remained strong, and the authorities were forced to take decisive action.

Several high-profile arrests were made, and the implicated officials and executives faced intense scrutiny. The government launched an independent inquiry into the corruption scandal, and Meridian Technologies faced significant consequences for its role in the scheme.

Throughout this period, Lisa remained steadfast in her commitment to the cause. With the support of her network, she continued to provide valuable information and guidance to Jake's team. Her courage and determination had made a significant impact, and she knew that the fight for justice was far from over.

## The Power of Solidarity

ONE EVENING, JAKE ORGANIZED a gathering of whistleblowers and advocates at a secure location. The goal was to foster a sense of solidarity and provide a platform for those who had come forward to share their stories and support each other.

As Lisa entered the room, she was struck by the diversity of the group. There were people from various backgrounds and professions, each with their own story of courage and determination. The atmosphere was one of mutual respect and solidarity.

Jake began the gathering with a few words of encouragement. "We're all here because we believe in the power of truth and the importance of accountability. Each of you has shown incredible bravery by coming forward, and together, we can make a difference."

Lisa listened as several whistleblowers shared their experiences. Their stories were a testament to the resilience of the human spirit and the impact that one person could have in the fight against corruption. As she listened, Lisa felt a renewed sense of purpose.

When it was her turn to speak, Lisa stood and addressed the group. "I want to thank each of you for being here. Your stories are inspiring, and your courage is a reminder that we're not alone in this fight. Coming forward was the hardest decision I've ever made, but it's also the most important. Together, we can bring about change and hold those responsible accountable."

The room erupted in applause, and Lisa felt a sense of solidarity and support that she hadn't felt before. The gathering was a powerful reminder that the fight for justice was not an individual endeavor but a collective effort.

## Building Momentum

AS THE INVESTIGATION continued to yield results, Jake and his team focused on maintaining the momentum. They worked closely with law enforcement to ensure that the evidence was thoroughly examined and that the implicated individuals faced legal consequences.

The public's support remained strong, with protests and rallies demanding accountability and transparency. The media coverage of the investigation was extensive, and the public's demand for justice showed no signs of waning.

One day, as Lisa was reviewing the latest developments with Jake and his team, they received a call from a prominent whistleblower advocate, Maria Lopez. Maria had been instrumental in several high-profile cases and was known for her relentless pursuit of justice.

"Jake, I've been following your investigation closely," Maria said. "You've done incredible work, and I believe that together, we can take this to the next level. I have contacts in the international whistleblower community who can provide additional support and resources."

Jake was thrilled by the offer. "Thank you, Maria. Your support would be invaluable. We're committed to seeing this through, and with your help, we can make an even greater impact."

With Maria's support, the investigation gained even more traction. The international whistleblower community rallied behind the cause, providing additional resources and amplifying the message. The fight for justice had become a global movement, and the pressure on the implicated entities continued to mount.

## A Turning Point

AS THE INVESTIGATION reached a critical juncture, Jake and his team prepared to publish their most explosive article yet. The article would reveal new evidence and testimonies that further implicated the key figures involved in the corruption scheme.

The night before the article was set to go live, Lisa received a call from Jake. "Lisa, we have everything we need. The evidence is irrefutable, and the public's support is stronger than ever. Tomorrow's article will be a turning point in our fight for justice."

Lisa felt a mix of excitement and apprehension. "I'm ready, Jake. Let's do this."

The next day, the article was published, and the response was immediate and overwhelming. The public's demand for accountability reached a fever pitch, and the authorities could no longer ignore the mounting evidence.

High-profile arrests were made, and the implicated officials and executives faced legal battles that would likely end their careers. The government enacted new regulations and oversight mechanisms to prevent future corruption, and Meridian Technologies faced significant consequences for its role in the scandal.

Throughout this period, Lisa remained steadfast in her commitment to the cause. Her courage and determination had made a significant impact, and she knew that the fight for justice was far from over.

One evening, as Lisa sat in her living room, she received a call from her parents. They had seen the news and were proud of her bravery and determination. Her younger brother, who had always looked up to her, expressed his admiration for her courage.

"We're so proud of you, Lisa," her mother said, her voice filled with emotion. "You've done something incredible, and we're here to support you every step of the way."

Lisa felt a sense of gratitude and relief. She had feared that her actions would alienate her from her family, but instead, they had brought them closer together. She knew that she had made the right decision, and she was ready to face whatever challenges lay ahead.

As she looked out at the city skyline, Lisa felt a renewed sense of purpose. The journey had been long and difficult, but she had emerged stronger and more determined than ever. She knew that the fight for justice was far from over, but she was ready to continue the battle, knowing that the truth had the power to change the world.

With Jake and her newfound allies by her side, Lisa embarked on the next chapter of her life. She was no longer just a mid-level employee at a government contractor—she was a symbol of courage and integrity, a whistleblower who had stood up against corruption and helped to bring about a new era of transparency and accountability. The road ahead was uncertain, but Lisa was ready to face it head-on, knowing that her actions had made a lasting impact and inspired others to do the same.

# Chapter 7: The Personal Toll

The relentless pursuit of justice had taken its toll on Lisa Bennett. The stress of her situation, combined with the constant threat of retaliation, was beginning to wear her down. As days turned into weeks, the personal cost of her courageous actions became increasingly apparent. The strain on her relationships, the isolation, and the ever-present paranoia were affecting every aspect of her life.

## Strain on Relationships

LISA SAT IN HER SMALL apartment, staring at her phone. It had been days since she last spoke with her family. The calls from her mother, once a comforting presence, had become increasingly frequent and concerned. Each conversation left Lisa feeling more anxious and guilty. She knew that her family was worried, but she couldn't tell them the full extent of what was happening. The secrecy was necessary, but it was also driving a wedge between her and the people she loved most.

One evening, Lisa finally picked up the phone and called her mother. The phone rang twice before her mother answered.

"Lisa, honey, is everything okay?" her mother's voice was filled with concern.

"Hi, Mom. I'm sorry I haven't called. Things have been really hectic at work," Lisa lied, trying to keep her voice steady.

"Hectic? Lisa, you've never been this distant before. What's going on? Your father and I are really worried about you."

Lisa felt a lump form in her throat. "I'm fine, Mom. Really. It's just... complicated right now. I promise I'll explain everything soon."

"Lisa, we love you. Whatever it is, we're here for you. Please, just let us help."

"I know, Mom. I love you too. I have to go now, but I'll call again soon. I promise."

As she hung up, Lisa felt a pang of guilt. The secrecy was necessary to protect her family, but it was tearing her apart. She missed them terribly, but the fear of putting them in danger kept her from reaching out.

Her friendships were also suffering. Once close-knit, her circle of friends had become distant. She avoided social gatherings and ignored invitations, afraid that her presence might bring unwanted attention. The isolation was suffocating, but Lisa knew it was the price she had to pay for her actions.

One of her closest friends, Rachel, had noticed the change. She called Lisa one evening, her voice filled with concern.

"Lisa, it's been ages. What's going on? You've been so distant lately."

"Hey, Rachel. I know, I'm sorry. Work has been crazy, and I've just been really busy," Lisa replied, trying to sound nonchalant.

"Busy? Lisa, we all have busy lives, but you've completely shut everyone out. Are you in some kind of trouble?"

Lisa hesitated, unsure of what to say. She wanted to confide in Rachel, but she couldn't risk it. "I'm okay, Rachel. Really. Just dealing with some stuff. I'll be back to my old self soon, I promise."

Rachel sighed. "I'm here for you, Lisa. Whatever it is, you don't have to go through it alone."

"Thanks, Rachel. I appreciate it. I'll call you soon."

As she ended the call, Lisa felt a deep sense of loneliness. She missed the camaraderie and support of her friends, but she couldn't risk involving them. The burden of her secret was heavy, and it was taking a toll on her mental and emotional well-being.

# Balancing Act

DESPITE THE PERSONAL strain, Lisa knew she had to maintain her job and cover her tracks while continuing to provide Jake with information. The dual life she was leading was exhausting, and the constant vigilance was wearing her down. Every day at work was a balancing act, trying to appear normal while secretly gathering evidence.

Lisa's role at Meridian Technologies involved managing compliance and ensuring that all projects adhered to federal regulations. Her position gave her access to critical information, but it also placed her under constant scrutiny. She had to be careful not to arouse suspicion while collecting documents and data.

One morning, Lisa arrived at the office early, hoping to retrieve some documents before her colleagues arrived. As she sifted through the files, she heard footsteps approaching. She quickly closed the drawer and turned to see her supervisor, Mr. Thompson, standing in the doorway.

"Good morning, Lisa," Mr. Thompson said, his tone friendly but curious. "You're here early. Everything okay?"

"Good morning, Mr. Thompson. Yes, everything's fine. Just catching up on some work," Lisa replied, trying to sound casual.

Mr. Thompson nodded. "I see. Well, keep up the good work. If you need anything, let me know."

As he walked away, Lisa let out a sigh of relief. The close call had rattled her, but she couldn't afford to be careless. She needed to be more cautious, but the pressure to gather evidence was mounting.

In the evenings, Lisa would meet with Jake and his team to review the information she had collected. These meetings were both a lifeline and a source of stress. They provided a sense of purpose, but they also reminded her of the dangers she faced.

One evening, as they sat in a dimly lit café, Jake reviewed the latest documents Lisa had brought. "This is good, Lisa. It corroborates what we've already found and adds more weight to our case."

Lisa nodded, but her exhaustion was evident. "It's getting harder to balance everything, Jake. The pressure at work, the secrecy, the isolation... it's all wearing me down."

Jake looked at her with concern. "I know it's tough, Lisa. But we're making progress. Every piece of evidence brings us closer to exposing the truth. You're not alone in this."

Lisa appreciated Jake's reassurance, but the weight of her double life was becoming increasingly difficult to bear. She felt like she was constantly walking a tightrope, and one misstep could bring everything crashing down.

# The Breaking Point

AS THE WEEKS PASSED, the strain on Lisa's personal life reached a breaking point. The constant vigilance, the isolation, and the fear of retaliation were taking a toll on her mental and physical health. She struggled to sleep, her nights plagued by nightmares and anxiety. Her performance at work began to suffer, and she found it harder to concentrate.

One afternoon, Lisa's supervisor, Mr. Thompson, called her into his office. She felt a knot of anxiety tighten in her stomach as she walked down the corridor. She knocked on the door and entered, her heart pounding.

"Lisa, have a seat," Mr. Thompson said, gesturing to the chair across from his desk. "I've noticed that you've been a bit distracted lately. Is everything okay?"

Lisa forced a smile. "I'm fine, Mr. Thompson. Just dealing with some personal issues. I'm sorry if it's affected my work."

Mr. Thompson leaned forward, his expression serious but sympathetic. "I understand that everyone has personal challenges, but I need you to be focused. We're under a lot of scrutiny right now, and we can't afford any mistakes."

Lisa nodded, her mind racing. "I'll do my best, Mr. Thompson. I appreciate your understanding."

As she left his office, Lisa felt a sense of dread. The pressure was becoming unbearable, and she feared that she was reaching her breaking point.

That evening, Lisa called Jake, her voice filled with anxiety. "Jake, I don't know how much longer I can keep this up. The pressure at work, the isolation, the constant fear... it's all getting to be too much."

Jake listened carefully, his tone reassuring. "Lisa, I understand. This is an incredibly difficult situation, but you're not alone. We're here to support you. If you need to take a step back, we'll find a way to manage."

Lisa took a deep breath, feeling a mix of relief and guilt. "I just don't want to let anyone down. But I'm not sure how much more I can handle."

"You're not letting anyone down, Lisa. You've already done so much. Your well-being is the most important thing. We'll work together to find a solution."

Jake's words provided some comfort, but Lisa knew that the challenges ahead would not be easy to overcome. The path she had chosen was fraught with danger and uncertainty, and the personal toll was becoming increasingly difficult to bear.

# Reaching Out for Help

DESPITE THE STRAIN, Lisa knew she couldn't give up. The fight for justice was too important, and she couldn't let the corrupt entities win. But she also knew she couldn't do it alone. She needed to find a way to balance her personal life and her role in the investigation.

One evening, as Lisa sat in her apartment, she decided to reach out to Dr. Karen Mitchell, the psychologist who had offered her support. She needed help coping with the stress and finding a way to manage her anxiety.

"Dr. Mitchell, it's Lisa," she said, her voice trembling. "I think I need to talk. The stress is getting to be too much."

Dr. Mitchell's voice was warm and understanding. "Of course, Lisa. I'm here to help. Let's schedule a session as soon as possible."

The counseling sessions with Dr. Mitchell provided a lifeline for Lisa. They gave her a safe space to express her fears and frustrations, and Dr. Mitchell helped her develop coping strategies to manage her anxiety.

"Lisa, it's important to take care of yourself," Dr. Mitchell said during one session. "You're facing incredible challenges, but you're also incredibly strong. Finding balance is key. Take time for self-care, and don't hesitate to lean on your support network."

Lisa nodded, feeling a sense of relief. "Thank you, Dr. Mitchell. I'll try to take your advice to heart."

In addition to the counseling, Lisa began to reconnect with her family and friends, albeit cautiously. She knew she couldn't share the full extent of what she was going through, but she needed their support.

One evening, she called Rachel, her close friend. "Rachel, I know I've been distant, and I'm sorry. I've been dealing with some things, but I miss you. Can we meet up sometime?"

Rachel's voice was filled with warmth. "Of course, Lisa. I've missed you too. Let's get together soon. Whatever it is, I'm here for you."

The reconnection with Rachel and her family provided a sense of normalcy and support that Lisa desperately needed. While she couldn't fully disclose her situation, the love and understanding from her loved ones helped her find the strength to continue.

# Finding Balance

WITH THE SUPPORT OF her network and the counseling from Dr. Mitchell, Lisa began to find a better balance in her life. She took steps to manage her stress and prioritize her well-being, while still contributing to the investigation.

At work, Lisa became more cautious and strategic in her actions. She took breaks to clear her mind and avoided staying late to minimize suspicion. She also found discreet ways to gather evidence, such as using secure communication channels and hiding documents in plain sight.

Jake and his team continued to work tirelessly, and the investigation gained more traction with each passing day. The public's demand for accountability remained strong, and the authorities were forced to take decisive action.

High-profile arrests were made, and the implicated officials and executives faced legal battles that would likely end their careers. The government enacted new regulations and oversight mechanisms to prevent future corruption, and Meridian Technologies faced significant consequences for its role in the scandal.

Throughout this period, Lisa remained steadfast in her commitment to the cause. Her courage and determination had made a significant impact, and she knew that the fight for justice was far from over.

One evening, as Lisa sat in her living room, she received a call from her parents. They had seen the news and were proud of her bravery and determination. Her younger brother, who had always looked up to her, expressed his admiration for her courage.

"We're so proud of you, Lisa," her mother said, her voice filled with emotion. "You've done something incredible, and we're here to support you every step of the way."

Lisa felt a sense of gratitude and relief. She had feared that her actions would alienate her from her family, but instead, they had brought them closer together. She knew that she had made the right decision, and she was ready to face whatever challenges lay ahead.

As she looked out at the city skyline, Lisa felt a renewed sense of purpose. The journey had been long and difficult, but she had emerged stronger and more determined than ever. She knew that the fight for justice was far from over, but she was ready to continue the battle, knowing that the truth had the power to change the world.

With Jake and her newfound allies by her side, Lisa embarked on the next chapter of her life. She was no longer just a mid-level employee at a government contractor—she was a symbol of courage and integrity, a whistleblower who had stood up against corruption and helped to bring about a new era of transparency and accountability. The road ahead was uncertain, but Lisa was ready to face it head-on, knowing that her actions had made a lasting impact and inspired others to do the same.

## Building a New Normal

AS LISA CONTINUED TO navigate her dual life, she gradually found ways to integrate her experiences into a new normal. She maintained her job at Meridian Technologies, becoming more adept at balancing her responsibilities while discreetly gathering evidence. The support from Jake's team, Dr. Mitchell, and her newfound allies provided a foundation of strength and resilience.

One day, as Lisa was working at her desk, she received an email from an anonymous source within the company. The email contained crucial information about another fraudulent project, along with instructions on where to find the relevant documents. Lisa's heart raced as she read the message. She knew this could be a significant breakthrough in the investigation.

That evening, Lisa met with Jake and the team to discuss the new information. "This could be the key to uncovering even more corruption," Jake said, his eyes filled with determination. "We need to follow this lead and see where it takes us."

With renewed energy, the team dove into the new evidence. They worked late into the night, cross-referencing the information with existing data and piecing together the puzzle. The results were astounding. The new documents revealed a network of shell companies and offshore accounts used to funnel money and hide illicit activities.

"This is incredible," Sarah said, her voice filled with excitement. "We have the smoking gun we've been looking for. This will make it nearly impossible for them to deny their involvement."

Jake nodded, his expression determined. "We need to prepare our next article carefully. This could be the turning point that finally brings them down."

As the team worked on the article, Lisa felt a sense of pride and accomplishment. Despite the personal toll and the challenges she had faced, her actions were making a difference. The evidence she had gathered, along with the information from the anonymous source, was helping to expose the corruption and bring about meaningful change.

## The Power of Community

AS THE INVESTIGATION continued to unfold, Lisa realized the importance of community and solidarity. She reached out to other whistleblowers who had come forward, offering her support and encouragement. The bond between them was strong, forged by shared experiences and a common goal.

One evening, Lisa organized a small gathering of whistleblowers at a secure location. The atmosphere was one of mutual respect and camaraderie. Each person shared their story, and the room was filled with a sense of solidarity and determination.

"Coming forward was the hardest decision I've ever made," Lisa said, addressing the group. "But knowing that I'm not alone has given me the strength to continue. Together, we can make a difference and hold those responsible accountable."

The gathering was a powerful reminder of the impact that individuals could have when they united for a common cause. The support and encouragement from fellow whistleblowers provided a sense of purpose and motivation for Lisa and others.

## Renewed Determination

WITH THE SUPPORT OF her network and the progress of the investigation, Lisa felt a renewed determination to see the fight for justice through to the end. The journey had been long and arduous, but she was more committed than ever to exposing the truth and bringing about change.

One evening, as Lisa sat in her living room, she received a call from Jake. "Lisa, we've done it. The authorities have enough evidence to move forward with indictments. The public's demand for accountability has reached a tipping point."

Lisa felt a surge of relief and pride. "That's incredible, Jake. We've come so far. Thank you for believing in me and supporting me through this."

Jake's voice was filled with warmth. "Thank you, Lisa. Your courage and determination have been the driving force behind this investigation. We're not done yet, but we're making a real impact."

As the weeks turned into months, the investigation continued to yield results. More high-profile arrests were made, and the implicated officials and executives faced intense legal battles. The government enacted new regulations and oversight mechanisms to prevent future corruption, and Meridian Technologies faced significant consequences for its role in the scandal.

Throughout this period, Lisa remained steadfast in her commitment to the cause. Her courage and determination had made a significant impact, and she knew that the fight for justice was far from over.

One evening, as Lisa sat in her living room, she received a call from her parents. They had seen the news and were proud of her bravery and determination. Her younger brother, who had always looked up to her, expressed his admiration for her courage.

"We're so proud of you, Lisa," her mother said, her voice filled with emotion. "You've done something incredible, and we're here to support you every step of the way."

Lisa felt a sense of gratitude and relief. She had feared that her actions would alienate her from her family, but instead, they had brought them closer together. She knew that she had made the right decision, and she was ready to face whatever challenges lay ahead.

As she looked out at the city skyline, Lisa felt a renewed sense of purpose. The journey had been long and difficult, but she had emerged stronger and more determined than ever. She knew that the fight for justice was far from over, but she was ready to continue the battle, knowing that the truth had the power to change the world.

With Jake and her newfound allies by her side, Lisa embarked on the next chapter of her life. She was no longer just a mid-level employee at a government contractor—she was a symbol of courage and integrity, a whistleblower who had stood up against corruption and helped to bring about a new era of transparency and accountability. The road ahead was uncertain, but Lisa was ready to face it head-on, knowing that her actions had made a lasting impact and inspired others to do the same.

## Embracing the Future

AS LISA LOOKED TO THE future, she felt a sense of hope and determination. The challenges she had faced had tested her limits, but they had also revealed her strength and resilience. She knew that the fight for justice was an ongoing journey, and she was ready to continue that journey with unwavering resolve.

One day, as Lisa was working at her desk, she received a message from Jake. "Lisa, we've been invited to speak at a national conference on whistleblowing and transparency. Your story has inspired so many, and I think it's time to share it with a wider audience."

Lisa felt a mix of excitement and apprehension. The thought of speaking in front of a large audience was daunting, but she knew that her story could inspire others to take a stand.

"Let's do it, Jake. If sharing my story can help others find the courage to come forward, then it's worth it."

The conference was a resounding success. Lisa's speech was met with standing ovations and heartfelt applause. Her story resonated with many, and she received numerous messages of support and gratitude from people who had been inspired by her courage.

As she stood on the stage, looking out at the faces in the audience, Lisa felt a sense of fulfillment and purpose. She had come a long way from the isolated and paranoid person she had once been. With the support of her allies and the strength of her convictions, she had transformed into a beacon of hope and integrity.

The road ahead was still uncertain, but Lisa knew that she was not alone. She had found a community of like-minded individuals who were committed to fighting for justice and transparency. Together, they would continue to make a difference and build a better future.

As Lisa left the conference, she felt a sense of peace and determination. She had faced incredible challenges, but she had emerged stronger and more resilient. She knew that the fight for justice was far from over, but she was ready to continue that fight with unwavering resolve.

With the support of her allies and the strength of her convictions, Lisa was ready to embrace the future. She was a symbol of courage and integrity, a whistleblower who had stood up against corruption and helped to bring about a new era of transparency and accountability. The road ahead was uncertain, but Lisa was ready to face it head-on, knowing that her actions had made a lasting impact and inspired others to do the same.

# Chapter 8: The Legal Battle

The investigation led by Jake Harrison and fueled by Lisa Bennett's courage had peeled back the layers of corruption at Meridian Technologies and implicated several high-ranking government officials. The public's demand for accountability had reached a fever pitch, and the authorities had been forced to take decisive action. But the powerful figures behind the corruption were not about to go down without a fight. In a desperate bid to suppress the truth, they launched a preemptive legal strike against Jake's publication, seeking court orders to stop the leaks and suing for defamation.

## Legal Maneuvering

THE FIRST SIGN OF THE impending legal battle came in the form of a thick envelope delivered to Jake's office. Inside was a detailed lawsuit filed by Meridian Technologies and the implicated officials. The lawsuit claimed that Jake's articles were defamatory, that they had caused irreparable harm to their reputations and businesses, and demanded immediate cessation of all further publications related to the investigation. The lawsuit also sought substantial damages, enough to potentially bankrupt the publication.

Jake's heart sank as he read through the document. This was a well-calculated move, a clear attempt to silence him and his team through intimidation and legal might. He immediately contacted Sarah, the legal expert who had been an invaluable ally throughout the investigation.

"Sarah, we've been hit with a lawsuit," Jake said, his voice tinged with urgency. "They're trying to shut us down and suppress any further leaks. We need to strategize our next move."

Sarah, ever the professional, quickly grasped the gravity of the situation. "This is a classic SLAPP suit—Strategic Lawsuit Against Public Participation. They're trying to intimidate us into silence. But we won't let them. I'll start preparing our defense and look into filing an anti-SLAPP motion. We have a strong case, and we need to make sure the court sees that."

Jake nodded, feeling a mix of anxiety and determination. "Thanks, Sarah. We need to fight this with everything we've got. The truth needs to come out, and we can't let them bully us into submission."

Sarah immediately went to work, assembling a team of experienced lawyers who specialized in media law and First Amendment rights. The legal team convened in a conference room, poring over the lawsuit and developing a strategy to counter the attack.

"We need to show that our reporting is based on verified evidence and that it's in the public interest," Sarah explained to the team. "We'll argue that the public's right to know about corruption and illegal activities outweighs any claims of defamation. We also need to prove that our sources are credible and that we conducted our investigation with due diligence."

The legal team worked around the clock, gathering evidence, reviewing legal precedents, and preparing arguments. They knew that this case would be a landmark battle for freedom of the press and the public's right to know. The stakes were incredibly high, not just for Jake's publication, but for the principles of transparency and accountability in journalism.

## Courtroom Drama

THE COURTROOM WAS PACKED on the day of the preliminary hearing. The atmosphere was charged with tension and anticipation. Journalists, activists, and members of the public filled the seats, eager to witness the high-stakes legal battle unfold.

Jake sat at the defense table with Sarah and the legal team, feeling a mix of nerves and determination. Across the aisle sat the plaintiffs—representatives of Meridian Technologies and the implicated officials, flanked by their high-powered attorneys. The contrast was stark: on one side, a team driven by a sense of justice and truth; on the other, a team motivated by power and the desire to protect their interests.

The judge, a seasoned and fair-minded jurist, called the court to order. The plaintiffs' lead attorney, a formidable figure known for his aggressive tactics, rose to address the court.

"Your Honor, we are here today because the defendants have engaged in a reckless smear campaign against my clients. Their articles are filled with baseless accusations, damaging the reputations of respected business leaders and public officials. We seek immediate injunctive relief to prevent further publications and to mitigate the harm already caused."

Sarah rose to respond, her demeanor calm but resolute. "Your Honor, this lawsuit is nothing more than an attempt to silence legitimate investigative journalism. The evidence we have presented in our articles is based on thorough investigation and verified sources. The public has a right to know about the corruption and illegal activities of those in power. We will show that our reporting is not only accurate but also essential for the public interest."

The judge listened intently, his expression neutral but attentive. "I will hear arguments from both sides. The burden is on the plaintiffs to prove that the publications are defamatory and not in the public interest."

Over the next several days, the courtroom became a battleground for the principles of free speech and accountability. The plaintiffs' attorneys presented their case, arguing that the articles had caused significant harm to their clients' reputations and businesses. They called witnesses who testified about the alleged damage, attempting to paint Jake's publication as reckless and irresponsible.

Sarah and her team countered with a robust defense. They presented detailed evidence supporting the claims made in the articles, including documents, financial records, and testimonies from whistleblowers. They argued that the reporting was conducted with due diligence and that the public had a right to know about the corruption that had been uncovered.

Lisa Bennett, the whistleblower whose courage had been instrumental in exposing the corruption, was a key witness for the defense. She testified about the evidence she had discovered and the risks she had taken to bring the truth to light. Her testimony was compelling and heartfelt, underscoring the importance of the investigation and the need for transparency.

"Ms. Bennett, why did you decide to come forward with this information?" Sarah asked during the direct examination.

Lisa took a deep breath, her voice steady. "I came forward because I couldn't stand by and watch the corruption and illegal activities continue. I knew the risks, but I believed that the public had a right to know. The truth needed to come out, and I felt it was my responsibility to help expose it."

The plaintiffs' attorneys attempted to discredit Lisa, questioning her motives and integrity. But Lisa remained composed, answering their questions with clarity and conviction. Her testimony resonated with the judge and the courtroom audience, highlighting the courage and integrity that had driven her actions.

As the hearing progressed, Sarah presented legal precedents and arguments that reinforced the importance of freedom of the press and the public interest. She cited landmark cases that had upheld the right of journalists to report on matters of public concern, even when powerful figures sought to suppress the truth.

"Your Honor, the role of the press is to serve as a watchdog, to hold those in power accountable," Sarah argued. "Our reporting has uncovered significant corruption and illegal activities that the public has a right to know about. Silencing us would not only undermine the principles of free speech but also allow the corruption to continue unchecked."

The courtroom drama reached its peak during the closing arguments. The plaintiffs' lead attorney reiterated their claims of defamation and harm, urging the judge to issue an injunction to stop further publications. Sarah, in her closing argument, passionately defended the principles of free speech and the public's right to know.

"Your Honor, this case is about more than just a lawsuit. It's about the fundamental principles of democracy and accountability. Our reporting is based on verified evidence and serves the public interest. We urge the court to uphold the values of transparency and free speech, and to reject this attempt to silence the truth."

The judge took the case under advisement, promising a decision in the coming days. The tension in the courtroom was palpable as both sides awaited the ruling.

# The Judge's Decision

DAYS TURNED INTO WEEKS as the legal battle raged on. The public followed the case closely, and the media coverage was extensive. The outcome of the case would have far-reaching implications for the principles of free speech and accountability in journalism.

Finally, the day of the judge's decision arrived. The courtroom was once again packed with journalists, activists, and members of the public. Jake, Sarah, Lisa, and the legal team sat at the defense table, their faces tense with anticipation.

The judge entered the courtroom, his expression serious. He took his seat and began to read his decision.

"After careful consideration of the evidence and arguments presented by both sides, this court finds that the plaintiffs have not met the burden of proof required to demonstrate that the publications were defamatory or that they caused irreparable harm."

The judge's words were met with a collective sigh of relief from the defense team. The tension in the room began to ease as the judge continued.

"The evidence presented by the defense demonstrates that the reporting was based on verified sources and conducted with due diligence. The public interest in exposing corruption and illegal activities outweighs the plaintiffs' claims of defamation."

The judge looked directly at the plaintiffs' attorneys. "The motion for injunctive relief is denied. The court upholds the principles of free speech and the public's right to know. The lawsuit is dismissed."

The courtroom erupted in applause and cheers. Jake and his team hugged each other, their faces filled with relief and joy. The decision was a resounding victory for freedom of the press and the principles of transparency and accountability.

## Moving Forward

THE VICTORY IN THE courtroom was a turning point in the investigation. With the legal threat neutralized, Jake and his team continued their work with renewed determination. The public's support remained strong, and the authorities pressed forward with their investigations and prosecutions.

High-profile arrests were made, and the implicated officials and executives faced intense legal battles. The government enacted new regulations and oversight mechanisms to prevent future corruption, and Meridian Technologies faced significant consequences for its role in the scandal.

Throughout this period, Lisa remained steadfast in her commitment to the cause. Her courage and determination had made a significant impact, and she knew that the fight for justice was far from over.

One evening, as Lisa sat in her living room, she received a call from Jake. "Lisa, we've done it. The court's decision has set a precedent for protecting investigative journalism and the public's right to know. Your bravery has been instrumental in this victory."

Lisa felt a surge of pride and gratitude. "Thank you, Jake. I couldn't have done this without you and the team. We've come so far, and there's still work to be done, but this is a significant step forward."

As the weeks turned into months, the investigation continued to yield results. More articles were published, each one revealing new layers of corruption and further implicating the key figures involved. The public's demand for accountability remained strong, and the authorities were forced to take decisive action.

Several high-profile arrests were made, and the implicated officials and executives faced legal battles that would likely end their careers. The government enacted new regulations and oversight mechanisms to prevent future corruption, and Meridian Technologies faced significant consequences for its role in the scandal.

## Embracing the Future

AS LISA LOOKED TO THE future, she felt a sense of hope and determination. The challenges she had faced had tested her limits, but they had also revealed her strength and resilience. She knew that the fight for justice was an ongoing journey, and she was ready to continue that journey with unwavering resolve.

One day, as Lisa was working at her desk, she received a message from Jake. "Lisa, we've been invited to speak at a national conference on whistleblowing and transparency. Your story has inspired so many, and I think it's time to share it with a wider audience."

Lisa felt a mix of excitement and apprehension. The thought of speaking in front of a large audience was daunting, but she knew that her story could inspire others to take a stand.

"Let's do it, Jake. If sharing my story can help others find the courage to come forward, then it's worth it."

The conference was a resounding success. Lisa's speech was met with standing ovations and heartfelt applause. Her story resonated with many, and she received numerous messages of support and gratitude from people who had been inspired by her courage.

As she stood on the stage, looking out at the faces in the audience, Lisa felt a sense of fulfillment and purpose. She had come a long way from the isolated and paranoid person she had once been. With the support of her allies and the strength of her convictions, she had transformed into a beacon of hope and integrity.

The road ahead was still uncertain, but Lisa knew that she was not alone. She had found a community of like-minded individuals who were committed to fighting for justice and transparency. Together, they would continue to make a difference and build a better future.

As Lisa left the conference, she felt a sense of peace and determination. She had faced incredible challenges, but she had emerged stronger and more resilient. She knew that the fight for justice was far from over, but she was ready to continue that fight with unwavering resolve.

With the support of her allies and the strength of her convictions, Lisa was ready to embrace the future. She was a symbol of courage and integrity, a whistleblower who had stood up against corruption and helped to bring about a new era of transparency and accountability. The road ahead was uncertain, but Lisa was ready to face it head-on, knowing that her actions had made a lasting impact and inspired others to do the same.

# Chapter 9: The Turning Point

The investigation into Meridian Technologies and the implicated government officials had already made waves, but the fight for justice was far from over. The corrupt network still had powerful allies and significant resources at its disposal. Yet, Jake Harrison and his team, fueled by Lisa Bennett's courageous whistleblowing, pressed on with unwavering determination. Little did they know that they were on the brink of a major breakthrough that would turn the tide definitively in their favor.

## Major Breakthrough

IT WAS A TYPICAL EVENING at Jake's office. The team was working late, as usual, sifting through mountains of documents and data, looking for that elusive smoking gun. Sarah, the data analyst, had been particularly engrossed in a set of financial records that seemed to hint at deeper connections than they had previously uncovered.

"Jake, you need to see this," Sarah called out, her eyes wide with excitement and a hint of disbelief. Jake walked over to her desk, where she had several documents spread out.

"What did you find?" Jake asked, peering over her shoulder.

Sarah pointed to a series of transactions that seemed innocuous at first glance. "Look here. These payments to a consulting firm called Vertex Solutions—they're frequent, substantial, and don't correspond to any actual services rendered. I cross-referenced the firm with some of the other shell companies we've identified, and guess what? Vertex Solutions is tied to a bank account that's been flagged for suspicious activity."

Jake's brow furrowed as he absorbed the information. "Okay, that's suspicious, but how does this connect to our top targets?"

Sarah leaned in, her voice dropping to a whisper. "The account is linked to Senator John Mitchell."

Jake's eyes widened. Senator Mitchell was one of the most powerful and respected figures in government, a man who had built his career on a reputation for integrity. If they could prove his involvement, it would be a seismic shift in the investigation.

"We need more than just these transactions," Jake said, his mind racing. "We need direct evidence that Mitchell was aware of and benefited from the corruption."

Mark, the seasoned investigator, joined them. "Leave it to me. I have a few contacts who might be able to help us dig deeper. If Mitchell is involved, there will be more evidence out there."

Over the next few days, Mark worked tirelessly, reaching out to his network of informants and leveraging every resource he had. His persistence paid off when one of his contacts, a former aide to Senator Mitchell, agreed to meet.

In a dimly lit café, Mark sat across from the former aide, a nervous young man named Eric. "Thank you for meeting with me," Mark said. "I know this isn't easy, but we need your help to expose the truth."

Eric glanced around nervously. "I can't believe I'm doing this. But you need to know—Mitchell isn't the man he pretends to be. I handled a lot of sensitive information during my time with him, and I saw things that didn't add up. Payments, favors, meetings with shady characters. I have some documents that might help you."

Eric handed Mark a folder filled with emails, memos, and internal notes. Mark leafed through them, his pulse quickening. This was it—the evidence they needed. The documents detailed clandestine meetings, payments funneled through shell companies, and explicit instructions from Mitchell to cover their tracks.

"Eric, this is incredible," Mark said, his voice filled with gratitude. "You're doing the right thing. We'll protect you and make sure this evidence is used to bring them down."

Back at the office, Mark shared the documents with Jake and the team. The atmosphere was electric as they reviewed the evidence. The emails and memos directly implicated Senator Mitchell, revealing his central role in the corruption scheme. This was the major breakthrough they had been working toward.

"Jake, this is it," Sarah said, her voice trembling with excitement. "This evidence is irrefutable. We need to go public with this as soon as possible."

Jake nodded, his mind already racing ahead. "We need to prepare our next article carefully. This will cause a media firestorm, and we need to be ready for the backlash. But we can't delay. The public has a right to know."

# Public Reaction

THE DECISION WAS MADE. The team worked around the clock, drafting the article and verifying every detail. They knew that once they published this piece, there would be no turning back. The stakes had never been higher.

The morning the article went live, the reaction was immediate and explosive. The headline blared across news sites and social media platforms:

### "Senator John Mitchell Exposed: Corruption and Fraud at the Highest Levels of Government"

THE ARTICLE DETAILED the evidence they had uncovered, including the transactions, the shell companies, and the direct involvement of Senator Mitchell. It included excerpts from the emails and memos, painting a damning picture of one of the most powerful men in government.

Within hours, the media frenzy reached a fever pitch. News networks picked up the story, broadcasting the revelations non-stop. Social media erupted with outrage and calls for Mitchell's resignation and prosecution. The hashtag #MitchellCorruption began trending worldwide.

Jake's phone rang incessantly with calls from journalists, news anchors, and public figures seeking interviews and comments. He gave carefully measured responses, emphasizing the importance of transparency and accountability.

"The evidence we have uncovered is irrefutable," Jake said in an interview with a major news network. "Senator Mitchell has betrayed the public trust, and it's time for him to be held accountable. The public deserves to know the truth, and we will continue to uncover and report it."

The public reaction was intense. Protests erupted outside government buildings and Meridian Technologies' headquarters, with people carrying signs that read "Justice for the People" and "End Corruption Now." The pressure on the government to take action was immense.

Senator Mitchell, who had been a towering figure in politics, found himself at the center of a firestorm. He held a press conference, vehemently denying the allegations and claiming that he was the victim of a smear campaign.

"These accusations are completely false," Mitchell declared, his face flushed with anger. "I have always served the public with honesty and integrity. This is a baseless attack on my character, and I will fight it with everything I have."

But the public was not convinced. The evidence presented in Jake's article was too compelling to ignore. Calls for Mitchell's resignation grew louder, and political allies began to distance themselves from him.

## The Government's Response

THE GOVERNMENT, UNDER immense pressure from the public and the media, announced an independent inquiry into the corruption allegations. The inquiry was tasked with investigating the evidence and determining the extent of the corruption.

Jake and his team continued to provide information to the authorities, working closely with law enforcement to ensure that the investigation was thorough and unbiased. The inquiry moved swiftly, driven by the public's demand for accountability.

As the investigation progressed, more high-profile arrests were made. The implicated officials and executives faced intense legal battles, and the scope of the corruption network became increasingly clear. The government enacted new regulations and oversight mechanisms to prevent future corruption, and Meridian Technologies faced significant consequences for its role in the scandal.

The pressure on Senator Mitchell continued to mount. The inquiry uncovered more evidence of his involvement in the corruption scheme, and his attempts to discredit the investigation fell flat. Political allies who had once supported him now called for his resignation, and his once-stellar reputation lay in tatters.

In a dramatic turn of events, Mitchell announced his resignation in a televised address. His face was drawn and weary as he addressed the nation.

"I have always served the public with the utmost dedication, but the allegations against me have made it impossible for me to continue in my role.

I am stepping down to allow the inquiry to proceed without distraction. I maintain my innocence and will fight to clear my name."

The resignation sent shockwaves through the political landscape. It was a moment of vindication for Jake and his team, a testament to the power of investigative journalism and the importance of holding those in power accountable.

## The Aftermath

WITH SENATOR MITCHELL'S resignation and the ongoing inquiry, the public's demand for accountability remained strong. The investigation continued to yield results, uncovering more layers of corruption and further implicating key figures involved.

Jake and his team published more articles, each one revealing new evidence and shedding light on the extent of the corruption. The public's support remained unwavering, and the authorities were forced to take decisive action.

Several high-profile arrests were made, and the implicated officials and executives faced intense legal battles. The government enacted new regulations and oversight mechanisms to prevent future corruption, and Meridian Technologies faced significant consequences for its role in the scandal.

Throughout this period, Lisa remained steadfast in her commitment to the cause. Her courage and determination had made a significant impact, and she knew that the fight for justice was far from over.

One evening, as Lisa sat in her living room, she received a call from Jake. "Lisa, we've done it. The public's demand for accountability has led to real change. Your bravery has been instrumental in this victory."

Lisa felt a surge of pride and gratitude. "Thank you, Jake. I couldn't have done this without you and the team. We've come so far, and there's still work to be done, but this is a significant step forward."

As the weeks turned into months, the investigation continued to yield results. More articles were published, each one revealing new layers of corruption and further implicating the key figures involved. The public's demand for accountability remained strong, and the authorities were forced to take decisive action.

## Embracing the Future

AS LISA LOOKED TO THE future, she felt a sense of hope and determination. The challenges she had faced had tested her limits, but they had also revealed her strength and resilience. She knew that the fight for justice was an ongoing journey, and she was ready to continue that journey with unwavering resolve.

One day, as Lisa was working at her desk, she received a message from Jake. "Lisa, we've been invited to speak at a national conference on whistleblowing and transparency. Your story has inspired so many, and I think it's time to share it with a wider audience."

Lisa felt a mix of excitement and apprehension. The thought of speaking in front of a large audience was daunting, but she knew that her story could inspire others to take a stand.

"Let's do it, Jake. If sharing my story can help others find the courage to come forward, then it's worth it."

The conference was a resounding success. Lisa's speech was met with standing ovations and heartfelt applause. Her story resonated with many, and she received numerous messages of support and gratitude from people who had been inspired by her courage.

As she stood on the stage, looking out at the faces in the audience, Lisa felt a sense of fulfillment and purpose. She had come a long way from the isolated and paranoid person she had once been. With the support of her allies and the strength of her convictions, she had transformed into a beacon of hope and integrity.

The road ahead was still uncertain, but Lisa knew that she was not alone. She had found a community of like-minded individuals who were committed to fighting for justice and transparency. Together, they would continue to make a difference and build a better future.

As Lisa left the conference, she felt a sense of peace and determination. She had faced incredible challenges, but she had emerged stronger and more resilient. She knew that the fight for justice was far from over, but she was ready to continue that fight with unwavering resolve.

With the support of her allies and the strength of her convictions, Lisa was ready to embrace the future. She was a symbol of courage and integrity, a whistleblower who had stood up against corruption and helped to bring about a new era of transparency and accountability. The road ahead was uncertain, but Lisa was ready to face it head-on, knowing that her actions had made a lasting impact and inspired others to do the same.

# Chapter 10: The Whistleblower's Identity

The investigation had reached a fever pitch, with public support surging and high-profile arrests being made. But the corrupt entities implicated in the scandal were not about to let their empire crumble without a fight. They knew that the whistleblower who had ignited the investigation was the linchpin. If they could discredit or eliminate her, they might still salvage their positions of power. Despite Lisa Bennett's best efforts to remain anonymous, her identity was about to be leaked, putting her life in immediate danger.

## Unmasking

It was a quiet evening when the first signs of trouble appeared. Lisa was at her safe house, going through some documents Jake had sent her for review. Her phone buzzed with a notification from an anonymous source. She frowned and opened the message, which contained a single line: "Your cover is blown."

A wave of dread washed over her. Lisa quickly called Jake, her voice trembling with urgency. "Jake, I just received a message. Someone knows who I am."

Jake's heart sank. "Lisa, stay where you are. I'll get to you as fast as I can. And don't open the door for anyone."

He hung up and immediately called Tom Reynolds, the former prosecutor and whistleblower advocate who had been coordinating Lisa's protection. "Tom, we have a situation. Lisa's identity has been compromised. We need to move her to a secure location immediately."

Tom didn't hesitate. "I'll get my team ready. We need to act fast. Meet me at the safe house."

Jake grabbed his keys and rushed out of his office, his mind racing. He knew that Lisa's life was now in grave danger. The powerful figures she had exposed would stop at nothing to silence her. As he drove, he called Sarah, the legal expert, and Emily, the journalist, to inform them of the situation and to get additional support.

Within minutes, Jake arrived at the safe house. He knocked on the door in the agreed-upon pattern to reassure Lisa that it was him. The door opened, and Lisa stood there, her face pale with fear.

"Jake, what are we going to do?" she asked, her voice shaky.

"We're moving you to a more secure location," Jake said firmly. "Tom and his team are on their way. We're going to make sure you're safe."

As they spoke, Tom and his security team arrived. Tom took charge, his demeanor calm and professional. "Lisa, we're going to take you to a secure facility where you'll be protected around the clock. We've got everything arranged. Let's move quickly."

The team packed up Lisa's essential belongings and escorted her to a waiting vehicle. The drive to the secure location was tense, with everyone on high alert. They knew that any misstep could be fatal.

# Protecting Lisa

THE SECURE FACILITY was a remote, well-guarded house equipped with state-of-the-art security systems. Tom's team had vetted the location thoroughly, ensuring that it was the safest place for Lisa. As they arrived, Tom's team conducted a sweep of the premises to ensure it was secure.

Once inside, Lisa was briefed on the security protocols. "You'll have round-the-clock protection," Tom explained. "We've set up surveillance and have guards stationed at all entry points. If you need anything, let us know immediately."

Lisa nodded, still trying to process the sudden upheaval. "Thank you, Tom. I appreciate everything you and the team are doing."

Jake stayed with Lisa to help her settle in. "Lisa, I know this is overwhelming, but we're doing everything we can to keep you safe. The investigation is still ongoing, and your safety is our top priority."

Lisa managed a weak smile. "I trust you, Jake. It's just... hard to believe this is happening."

As Lisa adjusted to her new surroundings, Jake and Tom worked tirelessly to ensure her security. They coordinated with law enforcement to provide additional protection and monitored any potential threats closely. The situation was precarious, but they were determined to keep Lisa safe.

# The Media Frenzy

MEANWHILE, THE LEAK of Lisa's identity had triggered a media frenzy. News outlets were abuzz with speculation about the whistleblower who had exposed the corruption scandal. Reporters camped outside Meridian Technologies' headquarters and government buildings, hoping for a glimpse of the elusive figure.

Jake and his team were bombarded with calls from journalists seeking confirmation and interviews. They decided to issue a statement, emphasizing the importance of protecting whistleblowers and condemning the leak.

"Lisa Bennett has shown incredible courage in coming forward with information that has exposed significant corruption," Jake said in the statement. "Her safety is paramount, and we will do everything in our power to protect her. We condemn the leak of her identity and urge the media to respect her privacy."

The public reaction was mixed. Many expressed outrage at the breach of Lisa's anonymity and voiced their support for her. Others, particularly those loyal to the implicated officials, seized on the opportunity to discredit her.

Senator John Mitchell, who had resigned in disgrace, held a press conference to denounce Lisa. "This so-called whistleblower has been part of a smear campaign against me and my colleagues. Her allegations are baseless, and I will fight to clear my name."

The attempt to discredit Lisa only fueled the media frenzy. Reporters dug into her background, trying to piece together her story. Jake and his team remained steadfast, providing support to Lisa and working to counter the negative narratives being spread.

# A Close Call

DESPITE THE HEIGHTENED security, the threat to Lisa's life was very real. One evening, as she sat in the living room of the secure house, she heard a noise outside. Her heart raced as she glanced at the surveillance monitors. A figure was moving towards the house, avoiding the cameras.

Lisa quickly called Tom. "There's someone outside. I can see them on the monitors."

Tom responded immediately. "Stay inside and lock the doors. We're on our way."

The security team sprang into action, converging on the house. They spotted the intruder and apprehended him before he could get any closer. The man was carrying a knife and a set of lock-picking tools.

Tom's face was grim as he debriefed Lisa. "This was a close call. We believe he was sent to harm you. We're tightening security measures and increasing patrols. You're safe now, but we need to remain vigilant."

The incident shook Lisa deeply, but it also strengthened her resolve. She knew that the fight for justice was dangerous, but she was determined to see it through.

# Rallying Support

IN THE WAKE OF THE attempt on Lisa's life, Jake and his team decided to rally public support for her. They reached out to prominent figures in the whistleblower and activist communities, seeking endorsements and statements of solidarity.

One of the first to respond was Maria Lopez, a renowned whistleblower advocate. She issued a powerful statement condemning the attempt on Lisa's life and calling for greater protections for whistleblowers.

"Lisa Bennett has shown extraordinary courage in exposing corruption at great personal risk," Maria said. "The attempt on her life is a stark reminder of the dangers whistleblowers face. We must stand with Lisa and ensure she receives the protection and support she needs."

The statement galvanized public opinion, and a groundswell of support emerged. Rallies and vigils were held in major cities, with people holding signs that read "Protect Whistleblowers" and "Justice for Lisa." The public's support provided a much-needed morale boost for Lisa and her team.

# Strengthening Resolve

DESPITE THE DANGERS, Lisa remained committed to the fight for justice. She continued to provide information and guidance to Jake's team, working from the secure location. The investigation pressed on, uncovering more layers of corruption and further implicating the key figures involved.

One day, as Lisa reviewed some documents, she received a call from Jake. "Lisa, we've made significant progress. The authorities are preparing to press charges against several high-ranking officials. Your evidence has been crucial in building the case."

Lisa felt a surge of pride and determination. "That's great news, Jake. I'm glad to be a part of this. Whatever it takes, I'm with you."

Jake's voice was filled with gratitude. "Thank you, Lisa. Your bravery has made all the difference. We're going to see this through to the end."

As the weeks turned into months, the investigation continued to yield results. More high-profile arrests were made, and the implicated officials and executives faced intense legal battles. The government enacted new regulations and oversight mechanisms to prevent future corruption, and Meridian Technologies faced significant consequences for its role in the scandal.

Throughout this period, Lisa remained steadfast in her commitment to the cause. Her courage and determination had made a significant impact, and she knew that the fight for justice was far from over.

## The Road Ahead

AS LISA LOOKED TO THE future, she felt a sense of hope and determination. The challenges she had faced had tested her limits, but they had also revealed her strength and resilience. She knew that the fight for justice was an ongoing journey, and she was ready to continue that journey with unwavering resolve.

One day, as Lisa was working at her desk, she received a message from Jake. "Lisa, we've been invited to speak at a national conference on whistleblowing and transparency. Your story has inspired so many, and I think it's time to share it with a wider audience."

Lisa felt a mix of excitement and apprehension. The thought of speaking in front of a large audience was daunting, but she knew that her story could inspire others to take a stand.

"Let's do it, Jake. If sharing my story can help others find the courage to come forward, then it's worth it."

The conference was a resounding success. Lisa's speech was met with standing ovations and heartfelt applause. Her story resonated with many, and she received numerous messages of support and gratitude from people who had been inspired by her courage.

As she stood on the stage, looking out at the faces in the audience, Lisa felt a sense of fulfillment and purpose. She had come a long way from the isolated and paranoid person she had once been. With the support of her allies and the strength of her convictions, she had transformed into a beacon of hope and integrity.

The road ahead was still uncertain, but Lisa knew that she was not alone. She had found a community of like-minded individuals who were committed to fighting for justice and transparency. Together, they would continue to make a difference and build a better future.

As Lisa left the conference, she felt a sense of peace and determination. She had faced incredible challenges, but she had emerged stronger and more resilient. She knew that the fight for justice was far from over, but she was ready to continue that fight with unwavering resolve.

With the support of her allies and the strength of her convictions, Lisa was ready to embrace the future. She was a symbol of courage and integrity, a whistleblower who had stood up against corruption and helped to bring about a new era of transparency and accountability. The road ahead was uncertain, but Lisa was ready to face it head-on, knowing that her actions had made a lasting impact and inspired others to do the same.

## Building a Movement

IN THE WEEKS FOLLOWING the conference, Lisa and Jake's team continued to build momentum. They launched a campaign to advocate for stronger protections for whistleblowers, working with lawmakers and activists to draft new legislation. The campaign aimed to create a safer environment for individuals like Lisa who risked everything to expose the truth.

One of the key initiatives was the establishment of a Whistleblower Protection Fund, designed to provide financial support and legal assistance to whistleblowers facing retaliation. The fund received donations from public figures, corporations, and ordinary citizens who believed in the cause.

Lisa became a prominent figure in the movement, speaking at events and sharing her story. Her experience resonated with many, and she became a symbol of hope and resilience. The public's support for whistleblowers grew, and the movement gained traction.

As the campaign progressed, Lisa and her allies worked tirelessly to ensure that the new legislation was passed. They met with lawmakers, testified at hearings, and mobilized public support. The pressure on the government to act was immense, and the movement's efforts began to pay off.

## A New Era of Transparency

ONE DAY, LISA RECEIVED a call from Jake. "Lisa, we did it. The Whistleblower Protection Act has been passed. It's a landmark victory for our movement."

Lisa felt a surge of pride and relief. "That's incredible, Jake. We've come so far. This is just the beginning."

The passage of the Whistleblower Protection Act marked a new era of transparency and accountability. The legislation provided robust protections for whistleblowers, ensuring that they could come forward without fear of retaliation. It also established mechanisms for independent investigations and oversight to prevent future corruption.

The success of the campaign was a testament to the power of collective action and the importance of standing up for what was right. Lisa's journey had been fraught with danger and challenges, but it had also been marked by incredible resilience and determination.

## Embracing the Future

AS LISA LOOKED TO THE future, she felt a sense of hope and determination. The challenges she had faced had tested her limits, but they had also revealed her strength and resilience. She knew that the fight for justice was an ongoing journey, and she was ready to continue that journey with unwavering resolve.

One day, as Lisa was working at her desk, she received a message from Jake. "Lisa, we've been invited to speak at an international conference on whistleblowing and transparency. Your story has inspired so many, and I think it's time to share it with a global audience."

Lisa felt a mix of excitement and apprehension. The thought of speaking in front of a large international audience was daunting, but she knew that her story could inspire others to take a stand.

"Let's do it, Jake. If sharing my story can help others find the courage to come forward, then it's worth it."

The international conference was a resounding success. Lisa's speech was met with standing ovations and heartfelt applause. Her story resonated with many, and she received numerous messages of support and gratitude from people around the world who had been inspired by her courage.

As she stood on the stage, looking out at the faces in the audience, Lisa felt a sense of fulfillment and purpose. She had come a long way from the isolated and paranoid person she had once been. With the support of her allies and the strength of her convictions, she had transformed into a beacon of hope and integrity.

The road ahead was still uncertain, but Lisa knew that she was not alone. She had found a global community of like-minded individuals who were committed to fighting for justice and transparency. Together, they would continue to make a difference and build a better future.

As Lisa left the conference, she felt a sense of peace and determination. She had faced incredible challenges, but she had emerged stronger and more resilient. She knew that the fight for justice was far from over, but she was ready to continue that fight with unwavering resolve.

With the support of her allies and the strength of her convictions, Lisa was ready to embrace the future. She was a symbol of courage and integrity, a whistleblower who had stood up against corruption and helped to bring about a new era of transparency and accountability. The road ahead was uncertain, but Lisa was ready to face it head-on, knowing that her actions had made a lasting impact and inspired others to do the same.

# Chapter 11: The Fallout

The major breakthrough in Jake Harrison's investigation had led to the resignation of Senator John Mitchell and a public outcry for justice. But the battle was far from over. As the dust began to settle from the explosive revelations, both the government and the corporate world faced unprecedented pressure to act. This chapter details the profound fallout from the investigation, highlighting the government's response and the corporate shake-up that ensued.

## Government Response

THE DAY AFTER SENATOR John Mitchell's resignation, the atmosphere in Washington, D.C., was charged with anticipation and tension. The public demand for accountability had reached a critical mass, and the government could no longer ignore the call for justice. Amidst the growing pressure, the President called an emergency meeting with key advisors and officials to address the situation.

The White House briefing room was packed with journalists eagerly awaiting the official response. The President stepped up to the podium, looking resolute and determined.

"Good morning. The recent revelations regarding corruption and illegal activities involving high-ranking officials and corporate executives are deeply troubling. The American people deserve transparency and accountability, and I am committed to ensuring that justice is served. Effective immediately, we are launching an independent, bipartisan commission to investigate these allegations thoroughly. We will leave no stone unturned in our pursuit of the truth."

The announcement was met with a flurry of questions from reporters, but the President maintained a steady tone. "This commission will have full authority to investigate and will report its findings directly to the public.

Additionally, several officials implicated in the recent reports will be suspended pending the outcome of these investigations."

As the press conference concluded, the mood in the room was one of cautious optimism. The government's swift response was a significant step towards restoring public trust. However, the road ahead was fraught with challenges.

Within hours of the President's announcement, the commission was formed. It comprised respected legal experts, former judges, and prominent figures from both major political parties. Their mandate was clear: investigate the corruption allegations, identify those responsible, and recommend appropriate actions.

## The Commission's Work Begins

THE COMMISSION SET up its headquarters in a secure government building, away from the political fray. The lead investigator, Judge Emily Carson, a retired federal judge known for her integrity and impartiality, took charge of the proceedings. Her reputation lent credibility to the commission's work.

Judge Carson convened the first meeting with the commission members. "Our task is monumental, but it is crucial. We must approach this investigation with diligence and fairness. The American people are counting on us to uncover the truth."

The commission began by reviewing the evidence presented in Jake's articles, cross-referencing it with public records and other sources. They issued subpoenas for documents and called witnesses to testify under oath. The investigation was exhaustive, involving late nights and long hours, but the commission was determined to get to the bottom of the corruption scandal.

One of the first actions taken by the commission was to summon Senator Mitchell and other implicated officials for questioning. The hearings were televised, drawing millions of viewers eager to see justice unfold.

Senator Mitchell, once a towering figure in politics, now sat at the witness table, his demeanor subdued. The commission members took turns questioning him about the transactions, meetings, and communications detailed in the evidence.

"Senator Mitchell," Judge Carson began, "the evidence suggests that you were directly involved in facilitating illegal payments and covering up fraudulent activities. How do you respond to these allegations?"

Mitchell, visibly shaken, struggled to maintain his composure. "I have always served with integrity. The accusations are part of a coordinated attack against me. I deny any wrongdoing."

The commission members were relentless in their questioning, presenting document after document that contradicted Mitchell's claims. The public watched as the once-powerful senator's defenses crumbled under the weight of the evidence.

As the hearings continued, other officials and executives implicated in the scandal were called to testify. Some cooperated, hoping for leniency, while others tried to deflect blame or deny involvement. The commission's work was painstaking, but it was crucial in uncovering the extent of the corruption.

## Corporate Shake-Up

WHILE THE GOVERNMENT was grappling with the fallout, Meridian Technologies, the corporation at the center of the scandal, was facing its own crisis. The revelations had sparked a massive backlash against the company, and the consequences were swift and severe.

The day after the major breakthrough in the investigation, Meridian Technologies' stock prices plummeted. Investors, spooked by the uncertainty and potential legal ramifications, began to pull their money out. The company's market value dropped by billions of dollars within hours.

At Meridian's headquarters, the atmosphere was one of chaos and panic. Executives held emergency meetings, trying to devise a strategy to mitigate the damage. CEO Richard Collins, one of the key figures implicated in the scandal, knew that his position was untenable.

"We need to address this head-on," Collins said during a tense board meeting. "We have to show the public and our investors that we are taking this seriously and making necessary changes."

The board decided to hold a press conference to announce immediate actions. Collins, flanked by other top executives, faced the press with a somber expression.

"Today, we are announcing significant changes at Meridian Technologies. Effective immediately, I am stepping down as CEO. Additionally, several other executives implicated in the recent reports are also resigning. We are committed to cooperating fully with the ongoing investigations and will take all necessary steps to restore trust in our company."

The announcement did little to stem the tide of negative publicity. News outlets continued to scrutinize every aspect of Meridian's operations, and the public's anger showed no signs of abating. Employees, fearful for their jobs, faced a barrage of questions from friends and family about the company's future.

# Internal Reforms

IN A BID TO SALVAGE the company's reputation and stabilize its operations, the remaining leadership at Meridian Technologies decided to implement sweeping internal reforms. They hired an external consulting firm to conduct a thorough audit of the company's practices and recommend changes.

The consulting firm's report was scathing. It highlighted a culture of complacency and unethical behavior that had allowed corruption to flourish. The report recommended a complete overhaul of the company's governance structures, stricter compliance measures, and enhanced transparency.

Meridian Technologies' new interim CEO, Susan Drake, took the recommendations to heart. She addressed the employees in a company-wide meeting, outlining the steps that would be taken to rebuild trust and ensure accountability.

"We are at a crossroads," Drake said, her voice firm. "The actions we take now will define our future. We are committed to making Meridian Technologies a model of integrity and transparency. We will implement the recommended reforms, cooperate fully with the investigations, and hold ourselves to the highest ethical standards."

The reforms included appointing an independent compliance officer, establishing an anonymous whistleblower hotline, and conducting regular ethics training for all employees. The company also pledged to donate a portion of its profits to organizations that promoted corporate responsibility and transparency.

While these steps were necessary and welcomed, the road to recovery was long and fraught with challenges. The company's reputation had been severely damaged, and it would take time to rebuild trust with investors, customers, and the public.

## The Commission's Findings

AS THE COMMISSION'S investigation progressed, it became clear that the corruption was more extensive than initially thought. The evidence uncovered not only implicated Senator Mitchell and executives at Meridian Technologies but also revealed a web of collusion involving other officials and corporate entities.

The commission held a press conference to present its preliminary findings. Judge Carson stood before a packed room of journalists, the gravity of the situation evident in her expression.

"Our investigation has uncovered a widespread network of corruption involving high-ranking officials and corporate executives. The evidence indicates that these individuals engaged in illegal activities, including bribery, fraud, and money laundering. We are working closely with law enforcement to ensure that those responsible are held accountable."

The commission's findings sent shockwaves through the political and corporate worlds. Several high-ranking officials were suspended, and more executives at Meridian Technologies and other implicated corporations resigned or were fired.

The public's demand for accountability continued to grow. Protests and rallies were held across the country, with citizens calling for systemic reforms to prevent such corruption from occurring in the future.

## Legal Proceedings

WITH THE COMMISSION'S findings in hand, law enforcement agencies moved swiftly to press charges against the implicated individuals. Senator Mitchell, Richard Collins, and several other officials and executives were arrested and charged with various crimes, including bribery, fraud, and conspiracy.

The legal proceedings were high-profile and closely watched by the public. The trials were set to be landmark cases in the fight against corruption, with the potential to set important legal precedents.

As the trials began, the prosecution presented a mountain of evidence, including financial records, emails, and testimonies from whistleblowers and other witnesses. The defense teams, well-funded and experienced, fought vigorously to challenge the evidence and protect their clients.

Lisa Bennett, whose courageous whistleblowing had sparked the entire investigation, was called to testify. Her testimony was a pivotal moment in the trials, providing firsthand insight into the corruption and the risks she had taken to expose it.

"Ms. Bennett," the prosecutor began, "can you describe the moment you realized the extent of the corruption at Meridian Technologies?"

Lisa took a deep breath, her voice steady. "I discovered a series of transactions that didn't make sense. As I dug deeper, I realized that these payments were part of a larger scheme involving bribery and fraud. I knew I had to come forward, even though it meant risking my career and safety."

Her testimony was compelling and credible, painting a vivid picture of the corruption and the lengths to which the perpetrators had gone to cover it up. The public followed the trials closely, eager to see justice served.

# A New Chapter

AS THE TRIALS PROGRESSED, the commission continued its work, recommending further reforms to address the systemic issues that had allowed the corruption to flourish. The government acted on these recommendations, passing new legislation to enhance transparency, strengthen oversight, and protect whistleblowers.

The Whistleblower Protection Act, which Lisa and her allies had campaigned for, was a key component of these reforms. The Act provided robust protections for individuals who came forward with information about wrongdoing, ensuring that they could do so without fear of retaliation.

Lisa, Jake, and their team were invited to the White House to witness the signing of the Act. It was a moment of triumph and validation for their tireless efforts. As they stood in the Oval Office, watching the President sign the legislation into law, they felt a profound sense of accomplishment.

"Today, we take a significant step towards ensuring transparency and accountability in our government and corporations," the President said. "This Act is a testament to the courage of individuals like Lisa Bennett, who risked everything to expose the truth. We owe them a debt of gratitude."

The signing of the Act marked the beginning of a new chapter in the fight against corruption. It was a powerful reminder of the importance of integrity, courage, and the collective effort to build a better future.

## Moving Forward

WITH THE LEGAL BATTLES and reforms underway, Lisa and her allies focused on building a sustainable movement for transparency and accountability. They continued to advocate for stronger protections for whistleblowers and worked to raise awareness about the importance of ethical practices in government and business.

Lisa became a prominent speaker at conferences and events, sharing her story and inspiring others to stand up for what was right. Her journey from a mid-level employee at a government contractor to a symbol of courage and integrity was a testament to the power of individual action and the impact it could have on the world.

Jake and his team continued their investigative work, uncovering new stories and holding those in power accountable. The publication thrived, bolstered by public support and the success of their landmark investigation.

As Lisa looked to the future, she felt a sense of hope and determination. The challenges she had faced had tested her limits, but they had also revealed her strength and resilience. She knew that the fight for justice was an ongoing journey, and she was ready to continue that journey with unwavering resolve.

One day, as Lisa was working at her desk, she received a message from Jake. "Lisa, we've been invited to speak at an international conference on whistleblowing and transparency. Your story has inspired so many, and I think it's time to share it with a global audience."

Lisa felt a mix of excitement and apprehension. The thought of speaking in front of a large international audience was daunting, but she knew that her story could inspire others to take a stand.

"Let's do it, Jake. If sharing my story can help others find the courage to come forward, then it's worth it."

The international conference was a resounding success. Lisa's speech was met with standing ovations and heartfelt applause. Her story resonated with many, and she received numerous messages of support and gratitude from people around the world who had been inspired by her courage.

As she stood on the stage, looking out at the faces in the audience, Lisa felt a sense of fulfillment and purpose. She had come a long way from the isolated and paranoid person she had once been. With the support of her allies and the strength of her convictions, she had transformed into a beacon of hope and integrity.

The road ahead was still uncertain, but Lisa knew that she was not alone. She had found a global community of like-minded individuals who were committed to fighting for justice and transparency. Together, they would continue to make a difference and build a better future.

As Lisa left the conference, she felt a sense of peace and determination. She had faced incredible challenges, but she had emerged stronger and more resilient. She knew that the fight for justice was far from over, but she was ready to continue that fight with unwavering resolve.

With the support of her allies and the strength of her convictions, Lisa was ready to embrace the future. She was a symbol of courage and integrity, a whistleblower who had stood up against corruption and helped to bring about a new era of transparency and accountability. The road ahead was uncertain, but Lisa was ready to face it head-on, knowing that her actions had made a lasting impact and inspired others to do the same.

# Chapter 12: The Final Push

The fight for justice had been long and arduous, but Lisa Bennett and Jake Harrison were more determined than ever. The recent successes—the passage of the Whistleblower Protection Act, the high-profile resignations and arrests, and the public's unwavering support—had strengthened their resolve. Yet, they knew the battle was far from over. As they prepared for the final push, they braced themselves for the most significant and potentially dangerous phase of their investigation.

## Closing In

IN A NONDESCRIPT OFFICE building in Washington, D.C., Jake and his team had set up a temporary headquarters. The atmosphere was electric with anticipation. They were on the verge of compiling the final pieces of their investigation, preparing for the biggest and most damning reveal yet. This final installment would expose the full extent of the corruption, implicating even more powerful figures and uncovering the systemic failures that had allowed such corruption to flourish.

Lisa sat at her desk, surrounded by stacks of documents, her laptop open and buzzing with activity. She had been working tirelessly, sifting through data, cross-referencing information, and compiling evidence. The stakes had never been higher, and the pressure was immense, but Lisa was driven by a deep sense of purpose.

Jake entered the room, carrying a fresh stack of documents. "Lisa, I think we've got it. These files contain the missing links we've been searching for. If we can corroborate this with the data we already have, it'll be the final nail in the coffin for those involved."

Lisa took the documents, her eyes scanning the pages. "This is incredible, Jake. It's exactly what we needed. Let's get to work and make sure everything is airtight."

The team worked around the clock, piecing together the evidence with meticulous care. Each new discovery brought them closer to the truth, and the picture that emerged was more damning than they had ever imagined. The corruption was deeper and more widespread than they had initially thought, involving a complex web of deceit, bribery, and illegal activities that stretched across multiple sectors.

Sarah, the legal expert, provided invaluable guidance, ensuring that their findings would hold up under scrutiny. "We need to be absolutely certain that every piece of evidence is verifiable and irrefutable," she advised. "The people we're up against are powerful and will stop at nothing to discredit us."

Emily, the journalist, prepared the narrative for the final reveal. "This story needs to hit hard and leave no room for doubt," she said. "The public deserves to know the full extent of what's been happening behind closed doors."

As the days turned into weeks, the team's efforts began to bear fruit. The final report was nearly complete, a comprehensive exposé that detailed the corruption from top to bottom. It included financial records, emails, internal memos, and testimonies from whistleblowers and witnesses. The evidence was overwhelming and undeniable.

## Preparing for the Worst

WHILE THE TEAM WORKED tirelessly to finalize their investigation, they also anticipated severe retaliation. The powerful figures they were about to expose would not go down without a fight. Lisa and Jake knew they needed to take steps to protect themselves and their allies.

Tom Reynolds, the former prosecutor and whistleblower advocate, had been instrumental in coordinating security measures. He met with Jake and Lisa to discuss the plan. "We're dealing with people who have a lot to lose," he said. "We need to be prepared for any eventuality."

The team established secure communication channels and encrypted their data to prevent unauthorized access. They also arranged for round-the-clock security for key members of the team, including Lisa and Jake.

Lisa's safe house was fortified with additional security measures, including surveillance cameras, alarm systems, and a dedicated security team. Tom coordinated with local law enforcement to ensure that they were ready to respond to any threats.

"Lisa, we're taking every precaution to keep you safe," Tom reassured her. "But we need you to stay vigilant and report anything suspicious immediately."

Lisa nodded, her resolve unwavering. "I understand, Tom. I'm ready for whatever comes. We can't back down now."

Jake also took steps to protect the publication and its staff. He implemented stricter security protocols and briefed the team on how to handle potential threats. "We're about to make some powerful enemies," he warned. "But we have the truth on our side, and we need to stay strong."

The team members were fully aware of the risks but remained committed to their mission. They had come too far to turn back now, and the final push was within reach.

## The Final Countdown

WITH THE INVESTIGATION complete, the team prepared for the public reveal. The final report was ready, and the publication's website was primed for the biggest release in its history. Jake coordinated with media partners to ensure that the story would receive widespread coverage, amplifying its impact.

The night before the release, the team gathered for a final briefing. The room was filled with a mix of tension and determination. Jake addressed the group, his voice steady but filled with emotion.

"We've worked tirelessly to get to this point," he began. "Tomorrow, we'll reveal the full extent of the corruption that's been hidden from the public for far too long. This is our chance to make a real difference and hold those in power accountable. I'm proud of each and every one of you for your dedication and bravery. Let's see this through to the end."

Lisa stood, her eyes meeting each member of the team. "We're about to make history," she said. "No matter what happens, remember that we've done the right thing. We've exposed the truth, and we've given a voice to those who were silenced. Thank you all for standing with me."

The team spent the rest of the evening making final preparations. They double-checked the security measures, reviewed the report one last time, and braced themselves for the storm that was about to break.

# The Big Reveal

THE MORNING OF THE release dawned with a sense of anticipation and urgency. The final report went live at exactly 8:00 AM, accompanied by a comprehensive article that summarized the key findings. The headline was bold and unambiguous:

## "The Full Extent of Corruption: Unveiling the Truth Behind Meridian Technologies and Government Malfeasance"

THE ARTICLE DETAILED the intricate web of corruption, including the involvement of top government officials, corporate executives, and other influential figures. It laid bare the systemic failures that had allowed such corruption to thrive and called for immediate action to address the issues.

The reaction was immediate and explosive. News outlets across the country picked up the story, broadcasting the revelations non-stop. Social media erupted with outrage and calls for accountability. The hashtag #EndCorruption trended worldwide within minutes.

Jake's phone rang incessantly with calls from journalists, news anchors, and public figures seeking interviews and comments. He gave carefully measured responses, emphasizing the importance of transparency and accountability.

"The evidence we have uncovered is irrefutable," Jake said in an interview with a major news network. "The public deserves to know the truth, and those responsible must be held accountable. We will continue to expose corruption and fight for justice."

The public reaction was intense. Protests erupted outside government buildings and Meridian Technologies' headquarters, with people carrying signs that read "Justice for All" and "No More Corruption." The pressure on the government to take action was immense.

# Retaliation and Resilience

AS ANTICIPATED, THE retaliation was swift and severe. The powerful figures implicated in the final report launched a concerted effort to discredit Jake, Lisa, and the entire investigation. They filed lawsuits, spread misinformation, and used their influence to try to suppress the story.

Lisa's life was once again in danger. Despite the heightened security measures, she received anonymous threats and experienced attempts to breach her safe house. Tom and his team worked tirelessly to ensure her safety, but the situation remained precarious.

One evening, as Lisa sat in her secure house, she received a chilling phone call. "You've gone too far, Lisa. You're going to regret this." The line went dead, leaving her shaken but resolute.

She immediately contacted Tom, who reassured her. "We're increasing security and coordinating with law enforcement. Stay strong, Lisa. We won't let anything happen to you."

The team also faced cyber-attacks and attempts to hack into their systems. Sarah and the IT team worked around the clock to defend against these attacks and protect their data.

Despite the threats and challenges, the team remained resilient. They knew that the truth was their most powerful weapon, and they were determined to see justice served.

## The Impact

THE FALLOUT FROM THE final report was profound. The public's demand for accountability reached a crescendo, forcing the government to take decisive action. The independent commission, which had been working tirelessly to investigate the allegations, released a comprehensive report that corroborated Jake's findings.

Several high-ranking officials and corporate executives were arrested and charged with various crimes, including bribery, fraud, and conspiracy. The trials were set to be landmark cases in the fight against corruption, with the potential to set important legal precedents.

The government also enacted further reforms to address the systemic issues uncovered by the investigation. These reforms included stricter oversight, enhanced transparency measures, and additional protections for whistleblowers.

Meridian Technologies faced a massive corporate shake-up. The company's stock prices continued to plummet, and more executives resigned or were fired. The new leadership, led by interim CEO Susan Drake, committed to implementing the recommended reforms and rebuilding the company's reputation.

# A New Beginning

WITH THE FINAL REPORT published and the legal proceedings underway, Lisa and Jake took a moment to reflect on their journey. They had faced incredible challenges and risks, but their efforts had led to significant change.

One evening, as they sat in the office, Lisa turned to Jake. "We did it, Jake. We've exposed the truth and made a real difference. I couldn't have done this without you and the team."

Jake smiled, his eyes filled with pride. "You're the real hero, Lisa. Your courage and determination have inspired so many. This is just the beginning. There's still a lot of work to be done, but we've shown that it's possible to stand up against corruption and win."

As they looked to the future, they knew that the fight for justice was far from over. But they were ready to continue the journey, armed with the truth and supported by a global community of like-minded individuals.

# Moving Forward

IN THE WEEKS FOLLOWING the final reveal, Lisa and Jake focused on building a sustainable movement for transparency and accountability. They continued to advocate for stronger protections for whistleblowers and worked to raise awareness about the importance of ethical practices in government and business.

Lisa became a prominent speaker at conferences and events, sharing her story and inspiring others to stand up for what was right. Her journey from a mid-level employee at a government contractor to a symbol of courage and integrity was a testament to the power of individual action and the impact it could have on the world.

Jake and his team continued their investigative work, uncovering new stories and holding those in power accountable. The publication thrived, bolstered by public support and the success of their landmark investigation.

As Lisa looked to the future, she felt a sense of hope and determination. The challenges she had faced had tested her limits, but they had also revealed her strength and resilience. She knew that the fight for justice was an ongoing journey, and she was ready to continue that journey with unwavering resolve.

One day, as Lisa was working at her desk, she received a message from Jake. "Lisa, we've been invited to speak at an international conference on whistleblowing and transparency. Your story has inspired so many, and I think it's time to share it with a global audience."

Lisa felt a mix of excitement and apprehension. The thought of speaking in front of a large international audience was daunting, but she knew that her story could inspire others to take a stand.

"Let's do it, Jake. If sharing my story can help others find the courage to come forward, then it's worth it."

The international conference was a resounding success. Lisa's speech was met with standing ovations and heartfelt applause. Her story resonated with many, and she received numerous messages of support and gratitude from people around the world who had been inspired by her courage.

As she stood on the stage, looking out at the faces in the audience, Lisa felt a sense of fulfillment and purpose. She had come a long way from the isolated and paranoid person she had once been. With the support of her allies and the strength of her convictions, she had transformed into a beacon of hope and integrity.

The road ahead was still uncertain, but Lisa knew that she was not alone. She had found a global community of like-minded individuals who were committed to fighting for justice and transparency. Together, they would continue to make a difference and build a better future.

As Lisa left the conference, she felt a sense of peace and determination. She had faced incredible challenges, but she had emerged stronger and more resilient. She knew that the fight for justice was far from over, but she was ready to continue that fight with unwavering resolve.

With the support of her allies and the strength of her convictions, Lisa was ready to embrace the future. She was a symbol of courage and integrity, a whistleblower who had stood up against corruption and helped to bring about a new era of transparency and accountability. The road ahead was uncertain, but Lisa was ready to face it head-on, knowing that her actions had made a lasting impact and inspired others to do the same.

# Chapter 13: The Climax

The moment had arrived. Months of relentless investigation, countless hours of sifting through documents, interviewing witnesses, and verifying facts had led to this point. Jake Harrison, Lisa Bennett, and their dedicated team were about to release the final article that would expose the full extent of the corruption and illegal activities they had uncovered. The stakes had never been higher, and the impact of their revelations would be felt across the nation.

## Explosive Revelation

THE TEAM HAD GATHERED in their makeshift headquarters, the air thick with anticipation and tension. The final article was ready to be published, and the weight of its contents was monumental. This was not just another report; it was a detailed exposé that would lay bare the corruption that had infiltrated the highest levels of government and the corporate world.

Lisa sat at her desk, her heart pounding as she reviewed the final draft one last time. The article was comprehensive, meticulously detailed, and supported by an overwhelming amount of evidence. Financial records, emails, internal memos, and testimonies from whistleblowers painted a damning picture of a network of corruption that had operated with impunity for years.

Jake walked over, placing a reassuring hand on her shoulder. "This is it, Lisa. Are you ready?"

Lisa took a deep breath and nodded. "Yes, Jake. Let's do this."

Jake signaled to Emily, who was in charge of the publication's website. "Go live," he said.

Emily clicked a few keys, and within moments, the article was online. The headline was bold and unambiguous:

## "Unmasking the Corruption: A Nation Betrayed by Its Leaders and Corporations"

THE ARTICLE BEGAN WITH an overview of the investigation, detailing the efforts of the team and the risks taken by whistleblowers like Lisa. It then delved into the specifics, exposing how government officials and corporate executives had conspired to defraud the public, launder money, and manipulate policies for their benefit.

The narrative was gripping and damning. It highlighted key figures such as Senator John Mitchell, former CEO Richard Collins, and other high-ranking officials and executives who had played central roles in the corruption scheme. Each revelation was supported by irrefutable evidence, leaving no room for denial or obfuscation.

Within minutes of the article going live, the website was inundated with traffic. Social media platforms exploded with reactions as people shared the article, expressing shock, outrage, and a demand for justice. The hashtag #UnmaskTheCorruption quickly began trending worldwide.

Jake's phone rang incessantly with calls from journalists, news anchors, and public figures seeking interviews and comments. He gave carefully measured responses, emphasizing the importance of transparency and accountability.

"The evidence we have uncovered is irrefutable," Jake said in an interview with a major news network. "The public deserves to know the truth, and those responsible must be held accountable. We will continue to expose corruption and fight for justice."

# Immediate Consequences

THE EXPLOSIVE REVELATION sent shockwaves through the government and corporate sectors. The public's demand for accountability was deafening, and the pressure on authorities to act was immense. Within hours, the first high-profile arrests were made.

FBI agents, armed with arrest warrants and accompanied by media cameras, descended on the homes and offices of the implicated individuals. Senator John Mitchell was among the first to be taken into custody, his once-commanding presence reduced to a figure of disgrace as he was led away in handcuffs.

Richard Collins, the former CEO of Meridian Technologies, was also arrested at his opulent mansion. As he was escorted to a waiting vehicle, reporters shouted questions, but Collins remained silent, his face a mask of defeat.

The arrests continued throughout the day, with more officials and executives being apprehended. The public watched in real-time as the once-powerful figures who had betrayed their trust were held accountable for their actions.

The wave of resignations that followed was unprecedented. Government officials and corporate executives who had been implicated in the scandal but not yet arrested chose to step down rather than face the growing backlash. The resignations created a ripple effect, leading to a significant reshuffling of leadership in both the public and private sectors.

The government, under immense pressure, announced the formation of a special task force to oversee the investigation and ensure that all implicated individuals were brought to justice. The task force, comprised of seasoned investigators and legal experts, was given broad authority to conduct its work.

The public's demand for accountability extended beyond the arrests and resignations. Protests erupted in major cities across the country, with citizens calling for systemic reforms to prevent such corruption from happening again. The protests were peaceful but powerful, a testament to the collective will of the people.

## The Trials Begin

AS THE DUST BEGAN TO settle from the immediate fallout, attention turned to the upcoming trials of the arrested individuals. The legal proceedings promised to be some of the most significant in recent history, with the potential to set important precedents in the fight against corruption.

Lisa was called to testify as a key witness. Her testimony was critical, as it provided firsthand insight into the corruption and the risks she had taken to expose it. The night before her first appearance in court, she felt a mixture of anxiety and resolve.

Jake visited her at her secure location to offer support. "Lisa, you've already done so much. Your testimony will be crucial, but remember, you're not alone in this. We're all behind you."

Lisa nodded, her determination unwavering. "Thank you, Jake. I'm ready."

The courtroom was packed on the day of Lisa's testimony. Journalists, legal experts, and members of the public filled the seats, eager to witness the proceedings. The atmosphere was charged with anticipation.

As Lisa took the stand, she felt a surge of confidence. She had faced incredible challenges to get to this point, and now she had the opportunity to make a lasting impact.

The prosecutor began the examination. "Ms. Bennett, can you describe the moment you realized the extent of the corruption at Meridian Technologies?"

Lisa took a deep breath and began to speak. "I discovered a series of transactions that didn't make sense. As I dug deeper, I realized that these payments were part of a larger scheme involving bribery and fraud. I knew I had to come forward, even though it meant risking my career and safety."

Her testimony was compelling and credible, painting a vivid picture of the corruption and the lengths to which the perpetrators had gone to cover it up. The defense attempted to challenge her credibility, but Lisa remained composed, answering their questions with clarity and conviction.

The public followed the trials closely, eager to see justice served. Each new revelation and piece of evidence presented in court further solidified the case against the accused.

## The Impact

THE IMPACT OF THE FINAL article and the subsequent trials was profound. The public's demand for accountability had been met with decisive action, and the legal system was working to ensure that those responsible were held to account.

The government enacted further reforms to address the systemic issues uncovered by the investigation. These reforms included stricter oversight, enhanced transparency measures, and additional protections for whistleblowers. The Whistleblower Protection Act, which Lisa and her allies had campaigned for, was a key component of these reforms. The Act provided robust protections for individuals who came forward with information about wrongdoing, ensuring that they could do so without fear of retaliation.

Meridian Technologies faced a massive corporate shake-up. The company's stock prices continued to plummet, and more executives resigned or were fired. The new leadership, led by interim CEO Susan Drake, committed to implementing the recommended reforms and rebuilding the company's reputation.

Susan addressed the employees in a company-wide meeting, outlining the steps that would be taken to rebuild trust and ensure accountability. "We are at a crossroads," she said, her voice firm. "The actions we take now will define our future. We are committed to making Meridian Technologies a model of integrity and transparency. We will implement the recommended reforms, cooperate fully with the investigations, and hold ourselves to the highest ethical standards."

The reforms included appointing an independent compliance officer, establishing an anonymous whistleblower hotline, and conducting regular ethics training for all employees. The company also pledged to donate a portion of its profits to organizations that promoted corporate responsibility and transparency.

While these steps were necessary and welcomed, the road to recovery was long and fraught with challenges. The company's reputation had been severely damaged, and it would take time to rebuild trust with investors, customers, and the public.

## Personal Reflections

IN THE AFTERMATH OF the explosive revelation and the immediate consequences, Lisa and Jake took a moment to reflect on their journey. They had faced incredible challenges and risks, but their efforts had led to significant change.

One evening, as they sat in the office, Lisa turned to Jake. "We did it, Jake. We've exposed the truth and made a real difference. I couldn't have done this without you and the team."

Jake smiled, his eyes filled with pride. "You're the real hero, Lisa. Your courage and determination have inspired so many. This is just the beginning.

There's still a lot of work to be done, but we've shown that it's possible to stand up against corruption and win."

As they looked to the future, they knew that the fight for justice was far from over. But they were ready to continue the journey, armed with the truth and supported by a global community of like-minded individuals.

# Moving Forward

IN THE WEEKS FOLLOWING the final reveal, Lisa and Jake focused on building a sustainable movement for transparency and accountability. They continued to advocate for stronger protections for whistleblowers and worked to raise awareness about the importance of ethical practices in government and business.

Lisa became a prominent speaker at conferences and events, sharing her story and inspiring others to stand up for what was right. Her journey from a mid-level employee at a government contractor to a symbol of courage and integrity was a testament to the power of individual action and the impact it could have on the world.

Jake and his team continued their investigative work, uncovering new stories and holding those in power accountable. The publication thrived, bolstered by public support and the success of their landmark investigation.

As Lisa looked to the future, she felt a sense of hope and determination. The challenges she had faced had tested her limits, but they had also revealed her strength and resilience. She knew that the fight for justice was an ongoing journey, and she was ready to continue that journey with unwavering resolve.

One day, as Lisa was working at her desk, she received a message from Jake. "Lisa, we've been invited to speak at an international conference on whistleblowing and transparency. Your story has inspired so many, and I think it's time to share it with a global audience."

Lisa felt a mix of excitement and apprehension. The thought of speaking in front of a large international audience was daunting, but she knew that her story could inspire others to take a stand.

"Let's do it, Jake. If sharing my story can help others find the courage to come forward, then it's worth it."

The international conference was a resounding success. Lisa's speech was met with standing ovations and heartfelt applause. Her story resonated with many, and she received numerous messages of support and gratitude from people around the world who had been inspired by her courage.

As she stood on the stage, looking out at the faces in the audience, Lisa felt a sense of fulfillment and purpose. She had come a long way from the isolated and paranoid person she had once been. With the support of her allies and the strength of her convictions, she had transformed into a beacon of hope and integrity.

The road ahead was still uncertain, but Lisa knew that she was not alone. She had found a global community of like-minded individuals who were committed to fighting for justice and transparency. Together, they would continue to make a difference and build a better future.

As Lisa left the conference, she felt a sense of peace and determination. She had faced incredible challenges, but she had emerged stronger and more resilient. She knew that the fight for justice was far from over, but she was ready to continue that fight with unwavering resolve.

With the support of her allies and the strength of her convictions, Lisa was ready to embrace the future. She was a symbol of courage and integrity, a whistleblower who had stood up against corruption and helped to bring about a new era of transparency and accountability. The road ahead was uncertain, but Lisa was ready to face it head-on, knowing that her actions had made a lasting impact and inspired others to do the same.

# Chapter 14: The Aftermath

The final article had been published, and the explosive revelations had sent shockwaves through the nation. High-profile arrests had been made, and a wave of resignations had swept through the government and corporate sectors. Now, the focus shifted to the legal proceedings and the personal journeys of those who had risked everything to expose the truth. The aftermath of their actions would shape their lives and the nation's future.

## Public Trials

THE PUBLIC TRIALS OF the corrupt officials and executives began in a highly charged atmosphere. The courtroom was filled with journalists, legal experts, and members of the public, all eager to see justice served. The proceedings were broadcast live, drawing intense media coverage and public interest.

The first trial to commence was that of Senator John Mitchell, whose fall from grace had been swift and dramatic. The prosecution presented a mountain of evidence, including financial records, emails, and testimonies from whistleblowers like Lisa Bennett. The case against Mitchell was strong, and the public was eager to see one of the most powerful figures held accountable.

Lisa took the stand early in the trial, her testimony a pivotal moment in the proceedings. The courtroom was silent as she recounted her discovery of the corruption and the risks she had taken to expose it.

"Ms. Bennett," the prosecutor began, "can you describe the moment you realized the extent of the corruption at Meridian Technologies?"

Lisa took a deep breath, her voice steady. "I discovered a series of transactions that didn't make sense. As I dug deeper, I realized that these payments were part of a larger scheme involving bribery and fraud. I knew I had to come forward, even though it meant risking my career and safety."

Her testimony was compelling and credible, painting a vivid picture of the corruption and the lengths to which the perpetrators had gone to cover it up. The defense attempted to challenge her credibility, but Lisa remained composed, answering their questions with clarity and conviction.

The public followed the trial closely, eager to see justice served. Each new revelation and piece of evidence presented in court further solidified the case against Mitchell. The prosecution's case was meticulously detailed, leaving little room for doubt about Mitchell's guilt.

As the trial progressed, more witnesses were called to testify, each adding to the damning evidence against Mitchell. The prosecution presented emails that showed direct communication between Mitchell and other conspirators, discussing how to launder money and cover up their tracks. Financial experts testified about the complex web of transactions designed to hide the illicit activities.

The defense team, well-funded and experienced, fought vigorously to challenge the evidence and protect their client. They attempted to discredit witnesses, including Lisa, and argued that the transactions were legitimate and that Mitchell had no knowledge of any illegal activities. However, the overwhelming evidence presented by the prosecution made it difficult for the defense to mount a convincing argument.

The climax of the trial came when the prosecution played a recording of a conversation between Mitchell and a co-conspirator, discussing how to handle a potential investigation. The recording, obtained through a whistleblower, left no doubt about Mitchell's involvement and intent.

As the trial drew to a close, the public waited with bated breath for the verdict. The jury deliberated for several days, carefully considering the evidence. When they finally returned, the courtroom was packed, and the tension was palpable.

The foreperson stood and read the verdict: "Guilty on all counts."

The announcement was met with a mixture of relief and satisfaction. Justice had been served, and one of the most powerful figures in the corruption scandal was held accountable. Mitchell was sentenced to a lengthy prison term, and the public's faith in the justice system was reaffirmed.

# Rebuilding Lives

WHILE THE PUBLIC TRIALS continued, Lisa, Jake, and other whistleblowers began the process of rebuilding their lives. The personal and professional fallout of their actions was significant, and each faced unique challenges.

## Lisa Bennett

LISA'S LIFE HAD BEEN turned upside down by her decision to blow the whistle on Meridian Technologies. While she had become a symbol of courage and integrity, the personal toll had been immense. She had faced threats, harassment, and isolation, but she remained steadfast in her commitment to justice.

With the trials underway and the initial wave of media attention subsiding, Lisa began to focus on rebuilding her personal life. She moved out of the safe house and found a new apartment in a quieter part of the city. The transition was difficult, as she still had to be cautious about her safety, but she was determined to regain a sense of normalcy.

One of the first steps Lisa took was to reconnect with her family. The strain of the investigation and the constant danger had created a rift, but now she had the opportunity to rebuild those relationships.

One evening, Lisa invited her parents to her new apartment for dinner. As they sat around the table, she felt a mix of nervousness and relief. "I'm sorry for everything I put you through," she said, her voice filled with emotion. "I had to do what was right, but I know it wasn't easy for you."

Her mother reached across the table and took her hand. "We're so proud of you, Lisa. You did the right thing, and we're here for you, no matter what."

Her father nodded, his eyes filled with pride. "You've always been strong, and you've shown incredible courage. We're glad to have you back."

The evening was a turning point for Lisa. The support of her family gave her the strength to move forward and continue her work as an advocate for transparency and accountability.

## Jake Harrison

JAKE'S ROLE IN THE investigation had solidified his reputation as a fearless journalist committed to uncovering the truth. The success of the investigation brought new opportunities, but it also came with its own set of challenges.

The publication thrived, bolstered by the public's support and the success of the landmark investigation. However, the constant pressure and the threats from powerful figures had taken a toll on Jake. He realized he needed to find a balance between his professional dedication and his personal well-being.

One afternoon, Jake met with Emily, the journalist who had worked closely with him throughout the investigation. They sat in a small café, reflecting on their journey.

"We've achieved so much, Jake," Emily said, taking a sip of her coffee. "But we need to take care of ourselves too. The stress and danger we faced—it's not sustainable."

Jake nodded, his expression thoughtful. "You're right, Emily. We've been running on adrenaline for so long. It's time to find a way to continue our work without burning out."

They discussed strategies for maintaining their investigative efforts while also prioritizing their mental and physical health. They decided to implement regular breaks, seek support from mental health professionals, and foster a work environment that encouraged open communication and self-care.

Jake also took steps to strengthen the publication's infrastructure, ensuring that the team had the resources and support they needed to continue their important work. He invested in security measures, both physical and digital, to protect the team from potential threats.

As the months passed, Jake found a new rhythm in his life. He continued to lead the publication with the same passion and dedication, but he also made time for personal interests and self-care. The balance he achieved allowed him to be more effective and resilient in his work.

## Other Whistleblowers

THE OTHER WHISTLEBLOWERS who had come forward during the investigation also faced significant challenges as they rebuilt their lives. Each had their own story of courage and sacrifice, and the aftermath of their actions required them to navigate complex personal and professional landscapes.

One of the key whistleblowers was Eric, the former aide to Senator Mitchell. His decision to come forward had been instrumental in exposing the corruption, but it had also led to threats and harassment. Eric had to relocate and change his identity to protect himself from retaliation.

Eric found solace and support in a community of whistleblowers and advocates who understood the unique challenges he faced. He became an active member of this community, using his experience to support others who were considering coming forward.

During a support group meeting, Eric shared his story with new whistleblowers. "Coming forward was the hardest decision I ever made, but it was also the most important. We need to stand together and support each other. Our voices can make a difference."

His words resonated with the group, and many found the courage to take the next step in their own journeys. The community provided a network of support, resources, and advocacy, helping whistleblowers navigate the challenges they faced.

# Legal and Systemic Reforms

THE IMPACT OF THE FINAL article and the subsequent trials extended beyond the courtroom. The government enacted further reforms to address the systemic issues uncovered by the investigation. These reforms included stricter oversight, enhanced transparency measures, and additional protections for whistleblowers.

The Whistleblower Protection Act, which Lisa and her allies had campaigned for, was a key component of these reforms. The Act provided robust protections for individuals who came forward with information about wrongdoing, ensuring that they could do so without fear of retaliation.

One of the significant outcomes of the Act was the establishment of an independent whistleblower protection agency. This agency was tasked with providing support and resources to whistleblowers, investigating claims of retaliation, and ensuring that those who exposed corruption were protected and valued.

Lisa was invited to join the advisory board of the agency, her experience and insight proving invaluable in shaping its policies and initiatives. She worked closely with other board members to develop programs that supported whistleblowers and promoted a culture of integrity and accountability.

"We need to create an environment where whistleblowers feel safe and supported," Lisa said during one of the board meetings. "Our work is not just about protecting individuals; it's about fostering a culture that values transparency and ethical behavior."

The agency launched several initiatives, including educational programs for government and corporate employees, outreach campaigns to raise awareness about whistleblower protections, and a confidential hotline for individuals seeking advice and support.

The impact of these reforms was profound. The culture within government and corporate sectors began to shift, with increased emphasis on transparency, accountability, and ethical behavior. The fear of retaliation diminished as more individuals felt empowered to come forward with information about wrongdoing.

## Personal Growth and Reflection

AS LISA, JAKE, AND the other whistleblowers rebuilt their lives, they also experienced significant personal growth. The journey they had undertaken had tested their limits, but it had also revealed their strength, resilience, and capacity for change.

Lisa found a new sense of purpose in her advocacy work. She continued to speak at conferences and events, sharing her story and inspiring others to stand up for what was right. Her journey from a mid-level employee at a government contractor to a symbol of courage and integrity was a testament to the power of individual action and the impact it could have on the world.

One day, as Lisa was preparing for a speech at an international conference, she received a message from a young woman who had been inspired by her story. The message read: "Your courage gave me the strength to come forward about corruption in my own workplace. Thank you for showing me that one person can make a difference."

Lisa felt a surge of pride and gratitude. Her journey had not been easy, but it had made a real difference in the lives of others. She knew that the fight for justice was an ongoing journey, and she was ready to continue that journey with unwavering resolve.

Jake also experienced personal growth as he balanced his professional dedication with his personal well-being. He found new ways to support his team and foster a work environment that prioritized mental and physical health. The balance he achieved allowed him to be more effective and resilient in his work.

Reflecting on the journey, Jake realized the importance of self-care and support networks. "We can't do this work alone," he said during a team meeting. "We need to take care of ourselves and each other. Our strength lies in our ability to support one another and stay resilient in the face of challenges."

The other whistleblowers, including Eric, also experienced personal growth as they navigated the aftermath of their actions. They found strength in their community and used their experiences to support others who were considering coming forward.

## Looking to the Future

AS THE NATION MOVED forward from the explosive revelations and the subsequent reforms, the impact of the investigation continued to resonate. The legal proceedings against the corrupt officials and executives set important precedents in the fight against corruption, and the reforms enacted by the government and corporate sectors fostered a culture of transparency and accountability.

Lisa, Jake, and the other whistleblowers remained committed to their advocacy work, knowing that the fight for justice was far from over. They continued to raise awareness, support whistleblowers, and hold those in power accountable.

One day, as Lisa looked out at the city skyline, she reflected on the journey she had undertaken. The challenges she had faced had tested her limits, but they had also revealed her strength and resilience. She knew that the road ahead was uncertain, but she was ready to face it head-on, knowing that her actions had made a lasting impact and inspired others to do the same.

Lisa's phone buzzed with a message from Jake. "Lisa, we've been invited to speak at a global summit on transparency and accountability. Your story continues to inspire, and it's time to share it with the world."

Lisa felt a mix of excitement and determination. The thought of speaking in front of a global audience was daunting, but she knew that her story could inspire others to take a stand.

"Let's do it, Jake. If sharing my story can help others find the courage to come forward, then it's worth it."

The global summit was a resounding success. Lisa's speech was met with standing ovations and heartfelt applause. Her story resonated with many, and she received numerous messages of support and gratitude from people around the world who had been inspired by her courage.

As she stood on the stage, looking out at the faces in the audience, Lisa felt a sense of fulfillment and purpose. She had come a long way from the isolated and paranoid person she had once been. With the support of her allies and the strength of her convictions, she had transformed into a beacon of hope and integrity.

The road ahead was still uncertain, but Lisa knew that she was not alone. She had found a global community of like-minded individuals who were committed to fighting for justice and transparency. Together, they would continue to make a difference and build a better future.

As Lisa left the summit, she felt a sense of peace and determination. She had faced incredible challenges, but she had emerged stronger and more resilient. She knew that the fight for justice was far from over, but she was ready to continue that fight with unwavering resolve.

With the support of her allies and the strength of her convictions, Lisa was ready to embrace the future. She was a symbol of courage and integrity, a whistleblower who had stood up against corruption and helped to bring about a new era of transparency and accountability. The road ahead was uncertain, but Lisa was ready to face it head-on, knowing that her actions had made a lasting impact and inspired others to do the same.

# The Enduring Legacy

THE LEGACY OF THE INVESTIGATION and the actions of Lisa, Jake, and the other whistleblowers continued to resonate long after the trials and reforms. Their courage and determination had not only exposed corruption but had also inspired a new generation of individuals committed to transparency and accountability.

Educational institutions began incorporating case studies of the investigation into their curriculums, teaching students about the importance of ethics, integrity, and the role of whistleblowers in society. Organizations and advocacy groups used the story as a powerful example of the impact that individuals could have in the fight against corruption.

Lisa and Jake continued to work together, using their platform to support whistleblowers and promote a culture of transparency. They collaborated with international organizations, sharing their insights and experiences to help shape policies and initiatives that protected and empowered those who came forward with information about wrongdoing.

The impact of their work was felt around the world. Whistleblowers in other countries found the courage to expose corruption, knowing that they were not alone and that there were networks of support available to them. Governments and corporations implemented new measures to foster a culture of transparency and accountability, inspired by the reforms enacted in the wake of the investigation.

Lisa's journey from a mid-level employee to a global advocate for transparency and accountability was a testament to the power of individual action and the impact it could have on the world. Her story continued to inspire and motivate others, showing that one person could indeed make a difference.

As Lisa looked to the future, she knew that the fight for justice was an ongoing journey. The road ahead was still uncertain, but she was ready to continue that journey with unwavering resolve. She had found her purpose, and with the support of her allies and the strength of her convictions, she was ready to embrace whatever challenges lay ahead.

Lisa stood as a symbol of courage and integrity, a beacon of hope for those who sought to expose the truth and fight for justice. Her actions had brought about significant change, and her legacy would endure as a reminder that the power of one could transform the world.

The fight for justice was far from over, but Lisa was ready to continue that fight with unwavering resolve. With the support of her allies and the strength of her convictions, she was ready to embrace the future, knowing that her actions had made a lasting impact and inspired others to do the same.

As Lisa left the summit and walked into the bright light of a new day, she felt a sense of peace and determination. She knew that the road ahead was uncertain, but she was ready to face it head-on, with courage and integrity as her guiding principles. The journey she had undertaken had revealed her strength and resilience, and she was ready to continue that journey, knowing that the fight for justice was an ongoing and noble endeavor.

Lisa Bennett, a whistleblower who had stood up against corruption and helped to bring about a new era of transparency and accountability, was ready to embrace the future, confident in the knowledge that her actions had made a lasting impact and inspired others to do the same.

# Chapter 15: The New Dawn

T he sun rose on a new day, casting its light over a nation transformed by
the courage of a few individuals who dared to stand against corruption.
The journey had been long and arduous, but the efforts of Lisa Bennett, Jake
Harrison, and their allies had sparked a movement that led to systemic changes
and a renewed commitment to transparency and accountability. As they
reflected on their journey, they knew that their actions had made a lasting
impact, and they faced the future with hope and determination.

## Systemic Changes

THE PUBLIC TRIALS AND the overwhelming evidence presented during
the investigations had left an indelible mark on the nation. The government,
recognizing the need for comprehensive reforms to prevent future corruption,
enacted a series of new laws and measures inspired by the whistleblowers'
courage and the public's demand for accountability.

One of the most significant reforms was the establishment of the
Independent Commission on Transparency and Accountability (ICTA). This
new body was tasked with overseeing the implementation of anti-corruption
measures, conducting regular audits of government and corporate entities, and
providing a platform for whistleblowers to report wrongdoing safely and
confidentially.

The ICTA was given broad powers to investigate allegations of corruption,
issue subpoenas, and recommend disciplinary actions. It was staffed by a diverse
group of experts, including legal professionals, former judges, and
representatives from civil society organizations. The commission's mandate was
clear: to ensure that corruption would no longer be tolerated and that those in
power would be held accountable.

Lisa was invited to serve as an advisor to the ICTA, her experience and
insights proving invaluable in shaping its policies and initiatives. She worked
closely with the commission's members to develop protocols for protecting

whistleblowers, ensuring that they could come forward without fear of retaliation.

"We need to create a culture of integrity and accountability," Lisa said during one of the commission's meetings. "Our work is not just about punishing wrongdoers; it's about preventing corruption from taking root in the first place."

The ICTA launched several initiatives, including educational programs for government and corporate employees, outreach campaigns to raise awareness about whistleblower protections, and a confidential hotline for individuals seeking advice and support. These measures aimed to foster a culture of transparency and ethical behavior, ensuring that future generations would inherit a system free from corruption.

In addition to the ICTA, the government enacted new laws to enhance transparency and oversight. The Transparency in Government Act required all government agencies to publish detailed reports on their operations, budgets, and decision-making processes. This measure aimed to increase public access to information and ensure that government actions were subject to scrutiny.

The Corporate Accountability Act introduced stricter regulations for corporations, mandating regular audits, transparent reporting of financial activities, and the establishment of internal compliance programs. Companies found to be in violation of these regulations faced severe penalties, including hefty fines and the possibility of criminal charges for executives.

The Whistleblower Protection Act, which Lisa and her allies had championed, was further strengthened to provide additional safeguards for those who exposed wrongdoing. The Act included provisions for financial compensation, legal support, and psychological counseling for whistleblowers, recognizing the personal and professional risks they faced.

The reforms had a profound impact on the culture within government and corporate sectors. Employees at all levels were encouraged to speak up about unethical practices, knowing that they had the protection and support of the law. The fear of retaliation diminished as more individuals felt empowered to report wrongdoing.

# Legacy of Courage

AS THE SYSTEMIC CHANGES took effect and the nation began to heal from the wounds of corruption, Lisa and Jake took time to reflect on their journey. They had faced incredible challenges and risks, but their unwavering commitment to the truth had brought about significant change.

One afternoon, Lisa and Jake met at a quiet park, a place where they often came to find solace and reflect. They sat on a bench overlooking a serene lake, the sunlight shimmering on the water's surface.

"We've come a long way, haven't we?" Lisa said, her voice filled with a mix of pride and nostalgia.

Jake nodded, his expression thoughtful. "We have. There were times when it felt like an uphill battle, but we never gave up. And look at what we've achieved."

They sat in comfortable silence for a moment, taking in the beauty of their surroundings. The journey they had undertaken had revealed their strength and resilience, and they knew that their actions had made a lasting impact.

"Our work isn't done, though," Lisa continued. "There will always be challenges, and we need to stay vigilant. But I'm hopeful. The changes we've seen—people are more aware, more engaged. They're not willing to tolerate corruption anymore."

Jake smiled. "You're right. The fight for justice is ongoing, but we've laid a strong foundation. And we've shown that individuals can make a difference."

Their thoughts turned to the many people who had supported them along the way. The whistleblowers who had come forward, the legal experts who had provided guidance, the journalists who had reported the truth, and the countless citizens who had demanded accountability. It was a collective effort that had brought about change, and Lisa and Jake were grateful for the community of allies they had found.

As they reminisced, Lisa's phone buzzed with a message. It was from a young woman named Clara, who had attended one of Lisa's speeches and been inspired to expose corruption in her own workplace. The message read: "Your courage gave me the strength to come forward. Thank you for showing me that one person can make a difference."

Lisa felt a surge of pride and gratitude. Her journey had not been easy, but it had made a real difference in the lives of others. She knew that the fight for justice was an ongoing journey, and she was ready to continue that journey with unwavering resolve.

## Looking to the Future

WITH THE SYSTEMIC CHANGES in place and the public's renewed commitment to transparency and accountability, the future looked promising. Lisa, Jake, and their allies continued their advocacy work, knowing that the road ahead was still uncertain but filled with possibilities.

One day, as Lisa was preparing for a speech at an international conference on transparency and accountability, she received a message from Jake. "Lisa, we've been invited to speak at a global summit. Your story continues to inspire, and it's time to share it with the world."

Lisa felt a mix of excitement and determination. The thought of speaking in front of a global audience was daunting, but she knew that her story could inspire others to take a stand.

"Let's do it, Jake. If sharing my story can help others find the courage to come forward, then it's worth it."

The global summit was a resounding success. Lisa's speech was met with standing ovations and heartfelt applause. Her story resonated with many, and she received numerous messages of support and gratitude from people around the world who had been inspired by her courage.

As she stood on the stage, looking out at the faces in the audience, Lisa felt a sense of fulfillment and purpose. She had come a long way from the isolated and paranoid person she had once been. With the support of her allies and the strength of her convictions, she had transformed into a beacon of hope and integrity.

The road ahead was still uncertain, but Lisa knew that she was not alone. She had found a global community of like-minded individuals who were committed to fighting for justice and transparency. Together, they would continue to make a difference and build a better future.

As Lisa left the summit, she felt a sense of peace and determination. She had faced incredible challenges, but she had emerged stronger and more resilient.

She knew that the fight for justice was far from over, but she was ready to continue that fight with unwavering resolve.

# Building a Movement

IN THE YEARS THAT FOLLOWED, Lisa and Jake continued to build on the momentum they had created. They launched a foundation dedicated to supporting whistleblowers and promoting transparency in government and business. The foundation provided legal assistance, financial support, and advocacy for individuals who exposed corruption, ensuring that they had the resources and protection they needed.

The foundation also worked to raise awareness about the importance of integrity and ethical behavior. They partnered with educational institutions to develop curricula that taught students about the role of whistleblowers in society and the impact of corruption. Through workshops, seminars, and public campaigns, they aimed to foster a culture that valued honesty and accountability.

Lisa became a sought-after speaker at international forums and conferences, sharing her story and the lessons she had learned. Her message was clear: one person could make a difference, and collective action was essential in the fight against corruption.

During one such conference, Lisa met a young activist named Javier, who had been inspired by her story to expose corruption in his own country. Javier faced significant risks, but he was determined to bring about change.

"Your story gave me the courage to stand up," Javier said, his voice filled with determination. "I know the road ahead is tough, but I'm ready to fight for justice."

Lisa felt a deep sense of connection with Javier. She offered her support and connected him with resources and allies who could assist him in his journey. "You're not alone, Javier. We're all in this together. Keep fighting, and know that your courage will inspire others."

The foundation's work had a ripple effect, empowering individuals around the world to take a stand against corruption. Whistleblowers from various countries found the support they needed to expose wrongdoing, and the movement for transparency and accountability grew stronger.

# A New Era

AS THE SYSTEMIC CHANGES continued to take root and the movement for transparency gained momentum, a new era emerged. Governments and corporations adopted more robust measures to prevent corruption, and the culture of accountability became more deeply ingrained in society.

The impact of the reforms was evident in the increased public trust in institutions. Citizens felt more confident that their leaders were acting in their best interests and that mechanisms were in place to hold wrongdoers accountable. The fear of retaliation diminished as more individuals felt empowered to report unethical practices.

The media played a crucial role in this new era, with investigative journalism thriving and holding those in power accountable. Publications like Jake's continued to uncover stories of corruption and wrongdoing, shining a light on issues that needed to be addressed.

Jake's publication thrived, bolstered by public support and the success of their landmark investigation. The team expanded, bringing in new talent and expertise to continue their work. They remained committed to the principles of integrity and transparency, knowing that their role was essential in maintaining a just and accountable society.

Lisa, Jake, and their allies remained at the forefront of the movement, their work evolving as new challenges and opportunities arose. They collaborated with international organizations, sharing their insights and experiences to help shape policies and initiatives that protected and empowered those who came forward with information about wrongdoing.

# A Legacy of Integrity

AS LISA LOOKED BACK on her journey, she felt a profound sense of fulfillment. The challenges she had faced had tested her limits, but they had also revealed her strength and resilience. She knew that her actions had made a lasting impact, and she was ready to continue the fight for justice with unwavering resolve.

Lisa stood as a symbol of courage and integrity, a beacon of hope for those who sought to expose the truth and fight for justice. Her actions had brought about significant change, and her legacy would endure as a reminder that the power of one could transform the world.

The fight for justice was far from over, but Lisa was ready to continue that fight with unwavering resolve. With the support of her allies and the strength of her convictions, she was ready to embrace the future, confident in the knowledge that her actions had made a lasting impact and inspired others to do the same.

As Lisa walked into the bright light of a new day, she felt a sense of peace and determination. She knew that the road ahead was uncertain, but she was ready to face it head-on, with courage and integrity as her guiding principles. The journey she had undertaken had revealed her strength and resilience, and she was ready to continue that journey, knowing that the fight for justice was an ongoing and noble endeavor.

Lisa Bennett, a whistleblower who had stood up against corruption and helped to bring about a new era of transparency and accountability, was ready to embrace the future, confident in the knowledge that her actions had made a lasting impact and inspired others to do the same. The legacy of her courage and integrity would endure, shaping a better, more just world for generations to come.

# Don't miss out!

Visit the website below and you can sign up to receive emails whenever Nicholas Andrew Martinez publishes a new book. There's no charge and no obligation.

https://books2read.com/r/B-A-HUIXB-SEXIF

**BOOKS 2 READ**

Connecting independent readers to independent writers.

# About the Author

Nicholas Andrew Martinez is a distinguished author known for his gripping political fiction. His novels delve into the intricacies of power, corruption, and intrigue, offering readers a thrilling and insightful look at the political landscape. With a background in political science and a passion for storytelling, Martinez crafts narratives that are both thought-provoking and suspenseful. Outside of writing, he enjoys analyzing current events, traveling, and engaging in civic discussions. Nicholas's work continues to captivate and challenge readers, cementing his reputation as a leading voice in political fiction.

Milton Keynes UK
Ingram Content Group UK Ltd.
UKHW030142051224
452010UK00001B/209